BUG BOY

ERIC LUPER

Bug Boy

FARRAR, STRAUS AND GIROUX
NEW YORK

Distributed in Canada by Douglas & McIntyre Ltd.
Printed in the United States of America
Designed by Jay Colvin
First edition, 2009
1   3   5   7   9   10   8   6   4   2

www.fsgteen.com

Library of Congress Cataloging-in-Publication Data
Luper, Eric.
    Bug boy / Eric Luper.— 1st ed.
        p.   cm.
    Summary: In 1934 Saratoga, New York, just as fifteen-year-old Jack
Walsh finally realizes his dream of becoming a jockey, complications
arise in the form of a female bookie, an unexpected visit from his
father, and a man who wants him to "fix" a race.
    ISBN-13: 978-0-374-31000-4
    [1. Horse racing—Fiction.   2. Jockeys—Fiction.   3. Gambling—
Fiction.   4. Sex role—Fiction.   5. Swindlers and swindling—
Fiction.   6. Fathers and sons—Fiction.   7. Saratoga (N.Y.)—
History—20th century—Fiction.]   I. Title.

PZ7.L979135 Bug 2009
[Fic]—dc22

                                                            2008026730

To the real Mr. Hodge, a true champion of children's literature

BUG BOY

Saratoga Race Course
Saratoga Springs, New York

Summer 1934

I

AFTER BEING COOPED UP IN THAT BOXCAR FROM Belmont to Saratoga, Fireside seems just about as desperate to run as I am to ride. That horse tugs at the reins in the hopes I'll let them loose, and he puffs like a steam engine each time his lead leg strikes the ground. Riding any racehorse for its first workout after traveling is like setting off a stick of dynamite—all that energy needing to get out.

And Fireside is no different.

Sure, it's the morning of opening day and all. Heck, everyone's excited. But Fireside is jumpier than usual and it makes me wonder if he knows something about this here racing season that I don't.

"Take that horse through his paces, Jack," Mr. Hodge calls to me from the rail. "I want him working hard at least six furlongs."

"Sure thing." I jerk my knees, and Fireside springs into a canter. You never work a horse hard the same day he's racing, but the down days are different. They say every extra pound a horse carries takes a length off at the finish line, and boy do they put on weight fast. You've got to keep them running or they get a belly on them. As far as I know, Fireside won't be competing for a few weeks, so it's extra important to keep him trim.

Fireside is the biggest and fastest horse I've ever had the chance to put my legs around. His sleek, gleaming coat is charcoal gray, nearly black, and his chest is as broad as the end of a barn. Despite his size, he's surprisingly nimble, able to skitter in and out of the pack like a sparrow darting between branches.

"Pick up the pace!" Mr. Hodge hollers, but I can't barely hear him. He's already long behind us, swallowed up by the morning mist. It's my favorite time of day, when the sun peeks over the tops of the pine trees and makes the fog look like a cloud decided to settle itself down on the track.

I give Fireside two taps with the whip and cluck in his ear. By my estimate, we cut two seconds off our next furlong. To top it off, Fireside's ears are still twitching, which means he ain't too serious about the run. This horse has a lot more to offer.

As we breeze past the next post, I give Fireside some slack. He takes every inch of those reins and really pours it on. Anyone who says that racing is cruel—that horses don't like digging down for that mile or so—has never been in the saddle of a world-class Thoroughbred as it's begging to tear down the stretch. Centuries of breeding's done it to them. Racing is in their blood. It's in their blood like it's in mine.

When we circle around to the backstretch, the only thing sparkling brighter than Mr. Hodge's pocket watch is his smile.

It makes the creases in his leathery face seem even deeper. "Great time, son," he calls as we gallop past.

Bucky, one of the other exercise boys and my best chum in the horse business, is waiting for me on the outside rail. He brings his pony alongside Fireside, and we loop back, making sure to get ourselves out of the way of other riders coming through. Sweat glistens on Fireside's withers. "You sure were moving there," Bucky says. "Let me guess. You were thinking about driving one of those Alfa Romeos in the Monaco Grand Prix."

"Actually, it was a Bugatti in the Belgian."

"It's always Bugattis with you."

"What can I say? I like Bugattis."

After we make our way back to Mr. Hodge, I wait for him to look up at me from his notes. "Fireside lifted his head again," I say. "He was doing the same thing back at Belmont, remember?"

Mr. Hodge takes off his felt fedora and picks invisible lint off it like he does every time he thinks hard on something.

"Given any more thought to that shadow roll?" I ask. A shadow roll is a fluffy pad that rests across the bridge of a horse's nose. It would block the lower part of Fireside's vision to keep him from getting spooked by shadows underfoot.

Mr. Hodge studies Fireside while he chews that cigar of his. The smoke smells like the applewood my family burns back home. "Fit him up for one," he says. "We'll make a champion out of that horse yet." Then he looks up at me. "And a jockey out of you."

That's just about the nicest thing Mr. Hodge has ever said

I smile so big he could stick a muck shovel in my ___ without it touching my cheeks. I snap the reins and head off the track alongside Bucky.

"Did you hear that?" Bucky bounces in his saddle like a puppy waiting to chase after a stick. "Mr. Hodge is gonna bump you up to jockey soon."

"He didn't say anything about soon."

"But someday," Bucky says. "Someday. Me, I'll be lucky to shine your riding boots."

"Don't talk down about yourself that way."

"Aw, you know it and I know it, Jack. I'm no better at riding horses than Fireside here is at knitting."

"Pipe down," I tell him. "Fireside's a good knitter. He made me a scarf last Christmas."

Bucky grins at that, and his two front teeth press down so hard I think he might bite his bottom lip clean off. With teeth like his, Bucky's nickname didn't take too much figuring out.

"I grew up on horseback," I say. "My grandpa used to tell me I came into the world holding the birth cord like it was a set of reins and I ain't stopped since."

The thought of my family makes my thighs tense up around my mount. I wonder what my baby sister, Penny, looks like now. I haven't seen her—or the rest of my family—in over three years, not since I was twelve and my dad sent me off with that rat Tweed McGowan to learn the horse business.

"The first thing you gotta do if you want to start riding better is raise those irons up," I say to Bucky, pointing to his stirrups. "You ain't never going to get comfortable if you keep riding Western like you do."

Bucky ignores me. "You watch," he says. "You'll be bumped

up to bug boy, win your first forty races right in a row, and be a full jockey in no time. Then, you'll forget all about the rest of us."

"How could I forget about you?" I say. "You owe me a quarter."

"A quarter? When you start riding for real, you won't bother stooping down for a crisp, new Ben Franklin, let alone a quarter. Things are going to take off for you, Jack. I can feel it."

"Does that mean I'm not getting my quarter?"

Fireside gives a little buck right then, and I hunch forward so as not to get tossed. I pat him on the neck and he seems to settle down some. When he bucks a second time, I know someone must be coming. Fireside gets jittery around strangers.

Then I see him.

In his gray suit and black fedora, the man is dressed too fancy to be a track worker. Even so, I can tell he ain't no pencil pusher. His nose is pushed in so bad it looks like he took a few too many shots to the snot locker. A few thousand too many.

"That's one fine horse you've got there," the man says.

One of the first things Mr. Hodge told me when I started working with Pelton Stables was never to converse with strangers who show up around the stable. He said folks like that are always looking for trouble. I nod to the man out of common politeness and guide Fireside to the far end of the shed.

"Yes, sir," the man continues as he trails alongside me. "That horse looks as sure as a Roosevelt dollar, he does."

As usual, Niles, Fireside's groom, is waiting for us. Niles always wears the same getup: a white, long-sleeved shirt and baggy pants with suspenders. He always wears the same eyes too—the kind that tell you his mouth is smiling just a few inches below. Even though I'm the one supposed to do it, Niles always hot-walks Fireside. He says the walking is as good for him as it is for the horse. Niles can say what he wants, but I'm glad to hand the bridle over. Leading a horse around and around in a circle until it cools down is a bigger bore than watching McIntoshes grow on the branch during a drought. Not to mention that all you need to do it is one good arm and the ability to turn to the left.

"Everything all right there, Mr. Jack?" Niles asks. His eyes flick toward the shifty guy.

"Fine," I say.

Niles helps me to the ground. After I thank him, I start toward the barn. Most of us workers sleep at local boarding-houses, but if there's a free stall at whatever track we're working, I take it. The chirping of the crickets and the snorting and stomping of the horses set me at ease.

When I get to my stall, I make sure everything is the way I left it. My unmade cot sits against one wall. Spoons, the spider monkey I picked up in a dice game down at Hialeah, is rolled up in the blankets, snoring away like an idling two-stroke engine. He has pulled off his black cap, but he's still wearing the purple and white striped silk jacket Mrs. Dalton, the boardinghouse keeper down in Belmont, made for him. Sure, that monkey is a pain in the keister, always stealing fruit and knocking things over, but his beady black eyes and the fuzzy ring of white fur around his wrinkled old-man face grow on you. Not to mention that he settles the horses down something serious.

The apple crate next to my cot is stacked high with things I like to look at before I go to sleep: old horse journal clippings, some car brochures, a few comic books, and some French postcards. I begin to straighten out the piles.

Someone clears his throat behind me. The phlegmy rattle sounds like one of those newfangled chain saws I saw at the fair ripping through a log. "So, what do you think of Fireside?" the guy in the suit says.

"Who are you?" I say right back. "You ain't even supposed to be back here."

He holds out his hand. "Name's Jasper Cunningham."

I don't want to shake on account of I don't trust the guy, so I spend some extra time taking off my helmet and hanging it on the hook I've nailed to the wall. The helmet's seen better days. The silk is frayed to bare threads, and the cardboard skullcap is tattered and soggy. Nevertheless, it was my first helmet and the thing's brought me nothing but good luck. And a new one costs two and a half bucks. Who's got that kind of money?

Jasper gets the hint and slips his hand back into his pocket. "Listen, kid," he says. His voice goes quiet and he steps toward me. "I know what life is like for you exercise boys. You're treated worse than these here horses. What are you, fourteen?"

I want to correct him, to tell him I'm fifteen, but I keep my mouth shut and take my good old time hanging up my crop. Neither of us says a word for a while, but being around the track so long, I know the sound of fingers riffling through cash.

I turn around.

Jasper's smile wrinkles that lump of a nose of his so bad it looks like a chewed up wad of gum. He knows he's got my attention. "Look, I have an offer for you, kid," he says, stepping close enough that he could grab me if he wanted. "I have an offer for you, and I think it's one you'll have a hard time turning down."

2

THE FIRST TIME I CAME UP TO SARATOGA, MR. HODGE
called Claire Court the Rolls-Royce of training tracks.
It's buried deep in the backstretch, behind the proper track,
behind rows of low barns and storage sheds. Huge oaks sur-
round the loop of white fencing as though the track was there
first, as though the trees themselves are the trespassers. I
hope Jasper doesn't ruin its charm for me, but as we walk over
there, I already know I'll never look at Claire Court the same
way again.

"Eat up," Jasper says, leaning against the fence. He nods to
the egg sandwich clutched in my hands. I haven't eaten much
these past few days, and all I want to do is shove that sandwich in my mouth. I want to swallow it in one bite and go get
me another.

The problem is I need to drop weight. I'm pushing one
hundred and sixteen pounds. That's a lot for a jockey. If a
chance to ride comes up and I'm not light enough, someone
else will get my mount. Mr. Hodge says I'm not ready for a big

race yet, but I'm lead exercise boy. Unless they hire on a seasoned rider to bump me, I'm the next one to move up.

Jasper takes a bite of his own sandwich. A chunk of egg
drops to the dirt. "I told you to eat up," he says. "I paid good
money for this grub."

I want to tell Jasper to chew and to swallow like a normal
human being, but thinking about eating makes my stomach
twist in knots. I unwrap the sandwich so an edge pokes out. If
I only eat the edge, I couldn't possibly gain weight. The smell
of scrambled eggs makes my eyes roll up so far I can nearly see
the wrinkles in my brain.

I take a small bite and tell myself to chew slowly, to savor
every moment the egg and cheese and roll are in contact with
my tongue.

Jasper still hasn't said a word about why he wants to talk,
but I figure I know. Owners try to hire experienced exercise
boys away from other stables all the time. That way, they get
fully trained riders instead of going through all the trouble of
teaching the ropes to new kids. A few of the other stables
have already offered, but I've turned them all down. Mr. Pelton and, more important, Mr. Hodge have been real good to
me. That's worth more than the few extra nickels I could
make someplace else. No one knows better than me how bad
getting with the wrong people can be.

I take another bite and swear it'll be my last. I can't afford
to gain an ounce. As Jasper inhales his sandwich—chewing
doesn't seem to be on his list of skills—a gray spotted gelding
gallops by. Its hooves sink deep into the dirt and kick up a
shovelful each time they lift out. The heavy surface of Claire
Court is perfect for building a horse's strength.

"Look, kid," Jasper finally says. "I'm not a bullshit kind of guy. I wanted to get you away from your barn so we could talk business."

Jasper pulls a cigar from his pocket and snips off the end with a small pair of scissors. He spins the cigar on his outstretched tongue until the dark leaf wrapper glistens with spit. He lights a match and puffs the cigar to life. "Fireside's going to be racing soon," he says. With each word, a small cloud of smoke pushes out of Jasper's mouth. It makes the smell of manure in the air seem even stronger. "When he does, I need you to make sure he doesn't win. Put simple, I need Fireside out of the picture."

My breathing goes shallow. "Out of the picture?"

Jasper smiles like he knows what I'm thinking. "Don't worry, kid. We just want him slowed up a little."

"I'm not Fireside's jockey," I say. "I only work him out."

"Don't you think I know that? But Showboat McGinn will stand to make a lot of dough if he wins on Fireside's back. We won't be able to sway him." Showboat McGinn is Pelton Stables's lead jockey and the guy likely to get to ride Fireside in any and all of his races.

"Who's we?" I ask.

Jasper chuckles through his nose, and it makes a squeaking sound. A fleck of snot fires out and lands on the edge of the white fence. If Jasper notices, he doesn't seem to care. "You don't think I'd tell you that, do you?"

I wrap the rest of my sandwich in the paper and perch it on the edge of the fence, well away from Jasper's snot. My fingers are covered in grease. I wipe them on my trousers.

"Here," Jasper says. He pulls out his handkerchief and

stuffs it in my hand. Normally I wouldn't take another guy's hankie, but judging from what's clinging to the fence post, I figure Jasper doesn't use his for wiping his nose.

"I don't think I can help you," I say. "Mr. Pelton's been good to me. I don't want to risk anything."

"Risk what?" Jasper says. "Sleeping in a stall with the horses every night? Getting treated worse than the animals you ride?" He leans in close, and his voice drops to a murmur. "Look, kid, we'll pay you two hundred dollars."

Two hundred dollars? Two hundred dollars is near two months' salary for regular folks. For an exercise boy, it's more like a million years' pay. With two hundred bucks I could go back home to the Finger Lakes for a while. I could see my sister. I could see my folks. I could visit Grandma's grave out by the orchard on the south hill.

But what would happen if I got caught? Exercise boys have been killed for much less than tampering with a horse. Not too long ago I heard a rider got beaten to death for lending a rival barn a few horseshoes. What would Mr. Hodge do if he found out I was messing with Fireside? What would Mr. Pelton do? My family depends on the small amount of money I send home every month. Thinking about little Penny makes up my mind for me.

"Sorry," I say. "I can't risk it."

"That's the beauty of it," Jasper says. "There *is* no risk." He reaches into his pocket and pulls out a round yellow sponge about the size of a skate wheel. He places it on the fence next to my sandwich. "On the day before the race, roll this up and stick it in one of Fireside's nostrils. Shove it in there deep so as you can't see it. It'll make it a little tougher for the horse to breathe. It'll slow him down just enough. No one'll be the wiser."

Jasper takes a white envelope out of his pocket and places it next to the sponge. I know there's two hundred dollars sitting in that envelope. All I have to do is take it. All I have to do is take the envelope and the sponge.

But the thought of doing anything to Fireside sours my stomach.

Not to mention that seeing that sponge makes me want to smack Jasper in his flattened face. It's not because he's asking me to do something low. Low things happen around the track all the time. It's because Jasper thinks he can make me do what he wants because of who he is and because of who I am.

I take a step away from the fence. Being near the money, like being near that egg sandwich, is too much of a temptation. I take another step back. "I'm afraid I can't help you, Mr. Cunningham."

Jasper nods but leaves the sponge and envelope on the fence. "Opportunities like this don't come along every day, kid."

"I'm sorry, but I just can't help you."

"It's not that you can't." Jasper lets his cigar drop from his fingers. He grinds it into the dirt with his heel and exhales a long stream of smoke that scatters on the breeze. "It's that you won't." He smiles, and just when I start to let my guard down, his hands fire out faster than twin bullets. He grabs my shirt and yanks my ear close. I can hear the worn fabric of my shirt tearing. I can smell the egg sandwich and stale cigar smoke. "There's something you should know about me," he says in a low growl. "I don't play around."

My hands clutch at Jasper's massive forearms. They're the forearms of a seasoned fighter, the forearms of a coal miner. Hell, those arms are steel girders. I'm too much of a chicken to pull away, so I dangle there in his grasp, hoping someone will come along and help me before Jasper pounds me into the ground like a railroad spike.

"I'll be around when you change your mind," he says. "And believe me—you're gonna change your mind." He lets go of me and snatches my egg sandwich from the fence. He unwraps it and takes a bite. "I figured you might be different. I figured you might have a head on your shoulders, but you're just as stupid as every other stupid breezer." With a second bite, Jasper finishes my sandwich. He lets the wrapper float to the ground. Another Thoroughbred, this one a young bay, gallops by and tramples the wrapper into the dirt. "Now, get the hell out of here," he says.

As he talks, bits of egg, cheese, and hard roll spray from his mouth, but I don't stick around long enough for them to come close to landing on me.

3

ON MY WAY BACK TO THE BARN, I START TO WONDER how long Jasper's had an eye on me. I rarely stay in a boardinghouse, and the thought that an ape like him could come into my stall any night he wants sends a tingle creeping up my back. The guy could've been watching since Belmont. Maybe longer. I push those thoughts from my mind and try to focus on the matter at hand: getting things ready for the season.

Considering it's our first day in Saratoga, things are pretty well organized. We move around so often we've gotten the hang of packing up one place and settling into the next. I made up the routine myself, and the guys have gotten pretty good at following orders. As I make my way up the shed row, I try to get Jasper out of my head by paying mind to every detail—making sure everything is just so. Each stall is stocked with water, hay, and a salt lick. The aisle along the barn is wide and clear. Fireside and all the other horses that worked out this morning are being hot-walked on the dirt circle in front.

Most important, the boys—who are a hundred percent my responsibility—are hard at work cleaning stalls.

As soon as Bucky sees me coming, he drops his shovel. The keys he always keeps hooked to his belt jingle like cowboy spurs with every step. "Where you been?" he asks.

"No place," I say.

"You're the one supposed to muck Fireside's stall. You made the chore list yourself."

"Sorry," I say. The funny thing is that I'd rather shovel ten tons of manure than spend two minutes with that Jasper guy. At least with manure you know what you're getting.

"It's like you up and disappeared," Bucky says.

"Just drop it, okay?"

"What's eating you?"

"Yeah," Oatmeal says. Oatmeal is one of the other exercise boys. He's busy brushing out a horse's mane. Oatmeal's face is more acne than skin, and his hair is wiry, like someone glued a giant S.O.S pad to the top of his head. "You look like you just seen a ghost."

"Everything's fine," I say.

"Suit yourself," Bucky says.

A couple workers lead Scotty Habana and Wild About Harry into their stalls and head off toward the main track.

Just then, Pug comes by with an old saddle slung over his shoulder. We call him Pug because he took a hoof to the face when he was a kid—at least that's what he tells us. His nose and upper lip got crushed so bad he resembles one of those dogs that looks like it got hit square in the snout with a golf club. It's not easy to understand him when he talks—it's more of a muffled kind of thing than actual words—but I've been around Pug long enough that I barely notice.

"What's eating you?" he asks me.

"Nothing!" I say. "Why don't you guys get off my back already?"

"Fine," Pug says. "I won't ask next time."

"Fine."

"Fine," Pug says again.

"Hey, whatcha got there?" Oatmeal asks, pointing to my hand.

I look down and realize I'm still holding Jasper's hankie. It hangs limp in my hand and is the only stark white thing on the shed row. I stuff it into my shirt pocket. "Nothing," I say.

"I'll bet some dame dropped her kerchief to Jack from the grandstand while he was trotting by," Oatmeal says. "Maybe she was some kind of princess." He snatches the hankie from my pocket. "Oh, Jack!" he calls in a high-pitched voice that sounds more like a rusty gate than a girl. "My father, the evil King Fat Cat, would disown me—maybe even throw me in the dungeon—if he found out my heart belongs to a mere stableboy, but take this token as a sign of my undying love!"

I try to snatch the handkerchief from Oatmeal's hand, but he tosses it over my head to Pug.

Pug begins walking around the stall on his toes, as though he's wearing high-heeled shoes. He thrusts his hips from side to side with every step and waves the hankie at me. "He wants for me to marry Sir Eldridge von Elkington so we can wed our struggling kingdoms, but I can't help who I love. I love you, poor stableboy! Jack Walsh, you're my hero!"

"Fine," I say. "If you guys want that hankie so bad, keep the damn thing. Maybe you three scrubs could use it to clean yourselves up."

"*Three?*" Bucky says. "I didn't do anything!"

"You didn't do anything to stop them either." I take a shovel and start mucking Fireside's stall where Bucky left off. My first shovelful lands with a heavy thud on the cart, and a screech drills my ears. Spoons the monkey darts out of the darkness of the cart onto a stack of crates. He hisses at me and starts scampering nervously from box to box, his purple and white jacket a blur.

Pug tries to hurl the hankie, but it only flutters and falls to the ground. "You boob," he mutters.

Without another word, we all get to work. Bucky starts hauling over fresh bedding from the straw pile. Oatmeal goes back to grooming. Pug drapes a saddle across his lap and starts polishing the cracked leather. It's so quiet, you could hear a tail hair hit the ground.

"Jack!" a voice booms. Spoons screeches again and leaps up to the rafters under the awning. "Jack, where are you hiding?"

It's Mr. Hodge. Could he have heard about Jasper so soon? I know better than to talk to folks who come around the stable asking questions. So what did I do? I went for a sandwich with the guy. It doesn't matter that I told him to go suck an egg. I know how this looks. Mr. Hodge is going to put his foot square in my can and not stop kicking until I'm in South Dakota. My racing career is going to be over before it begins.

Mr. Hodge rounds the corner of the barn like there's a fire that needs fighting. I stand to attention, ready to take whatever it is I have coming. I wonder if I have enough stashed away for train fare back to Syracuse or if I'll have to get the boys to throw some money together for me. Mr. Hodge strides across the shed row and hulks over me, but his expression looks nothing like I expect.

"Son, we have to get you spiffed up," he says. "Mr. Pelton wants you up in the box, posthaste."

Bucky gasps. Pug and Oatmeal stop their work and stare. Their jaws hang wider than a busted paddock gate.

"In his box?" I ask. "Up in the clubhouse?"

"What other box would I be talking about? His hatbox?"

I've never been in the clubhouse at any of the fancy tracks where we race. A box in Saratoga's clubhouse costs almost six dollars. That's more than a week's pay for me. Mr. Pelton's got a great spot right near the finish line—right next to the Rockefellers, the Whitneys, the du Ponts, the Vanderbilts, the Fitzsimmonses, and all those other high-society fat cats— but he's never called me up to it before.

"What's he want?" I say.

"It ain't my place to ask," Mr. Hodge says. "It's my place to do. Now what have you got to wear, son?"

"Nothing but work clothes."

Mr. Hodge's eyes narrow as though my lack of proper at- tire is a challenge. "Let me see what I can rustle up," he says. "In the meantime, see what you can do about making yourself look a little less like a rat that got run through a clothes wringer."

As soon as Mr. Hodge leaves, Bucky, Oatmeal, and Pug swarm around me as though we weren't just taking potshots at each other. I strip to my drawers and grab my towel.

"What do you think he wants?" Oatmeal asks.

"No idea." The dread in my voice rings louder than a church bell after a funeral service. No one wants to get called to the box. Especially on opening day. It means something big is happening. Something really big. Around the track, big changes for the good can be bad. Big changes for the bad can be terrible. Better to let things happen slowly, easily.

"I bet Mr. Pelton's gonna ask you to ride," Pug says.

"He wouldn't go to all the trouble of calling me up to the box for that. He'd have just told Mr. Hodge to tell me."

"That's true," Bucky says. "Maybe he wants to ask you something about one of the horses running today. Everyone knows how close you watch them."

I shrug. "Maybe."

The boys start running through all our horses' names, offering their opinions on each. I don't hear a single one of them. I can't get the idea out of my head that Mr. Pelton knows about Jasper and that I'm headed off the shed row for the last time. If there could be anything worse than me getting sent to the glue factory by Mr. Pelton, it'd be me getting sent to the glue factory by Mr. Pelton in front of all the other owners. After something like that, my chances of ever becoming a jockey would be over and done with. I'd be blacklisted.

I didn't do anything wrong, I say to myself. *I told Jasper to take a hike.*

On the train ride here, on the Cavanagh Special, one of the jockeys from White Birch Stables told me the Saratoga Sewing Club mends clothes at the Parish House for free. I haven't had a chance to get down there yet. We only pulled into town yesterday. At least I made the time to get myself a hot shower and really scrub myself clean at the YMCA last night.

I pull out my valise and rummage through it. My clothes are all rags. I've long since grown out of anything nice I had from home, and the hand-me-downs from other exercise boys are all in the sorriest of sorry shape. I grab the better of my two white shirts and the trousers with the smallest holes and begin unbuttoning my suspenders from my work pants. The minute I get my hands on any money, I'm going to buy myself some new duds—at least one good pair of trousers and a nice shirt—something that won't make me feel like a rail-riding hobo.

I dunk my head in Fireside's trough. The water is luke-warm, but it's cooler than the July air. By the time I towel off, slick back my hair, and put on my clothes, Mr. Hodge is back. He tosses me a tweed jacket. It smacks into my chest and drops to my hands. My fingernails are caked with grime.

"This is one of Showboat's," Mr. Hodge says. "Find a way to make it fit."

Jim "Showboat" McGinn is Mr. Pelton's star rider. Around here, he gets all the best mounts. For the longest time I kissed the shiny part of Showboat's ass, hoping to get promoted to apprentice sooner. No such luck. After a few months of polishing his saddles and boots until I could see my reflection, I found out Showboat told Mr. Hodge I had a bum shoulder and that he should keep me off the better horses.

Showboat is smaller than me, and I envy him for it. Among jockeys, small is good. Small is better than good; it's essential. His jacket is hot and scratchy, certainly not the right piece of clothing for a summer afternoon, but who am I to complain? It's worlds nicer than anything I've got. The fabric pulls taut across my back, and I can barely fasten the button. If I keep my arms at my sides, though, I figure I can pass for a guy who doesn't shovel horse manure for a living.

"You look great," Bucky says. He steers me outside, where Mr. Hodge is waiting.

"Yeah," adds Pug. He tucks Jasper's handkerchief into my breast pocket. "You're a real looker."

"Get on up there," Oatmeal says. "Don't keep the big man waiting."

"Guys . . ."

They all stare at me.

I wonder if this is the last I'll see of them. If I get fired, security guards might escort me right off the racing grounds, no coming back. In case it is, I should say something important. I should say something about how no matter what happens up in that clubhouse—regardless of if I get shitcanned and never come back—the three of them really matter to me.

"See you crumbs later." It's the best I can manage.

4

Even though I've been around racetracks every day for close to three years, the sound of the bugler playing the Call to Post still sends catfish wriggling up my spine. It's clear that the crowd feels the same way, because when that guy in the red velvet topcoat and stovepipe hat finishes tooting his horn, a cheer spreads from the grandstand to the picnic grounds that could bring John Dillinger's lead-filled body back from the grave.

Mr. Hodge leads me to the clubhouse. We take the stairs two at a time, and he tips his fedora to the usher who waves us past. "I'm sure I don't have to tell you this," Mr. Hodge says, "but you'd best be on par up there in that box. You do know what being on par means, don't you?"

"Par," I say. "Isn't that a golf thing? I'm not too keen on golf."

"It's got nothing to do with golf." He counts the words off on his fingers. "Polite. Accommodating. Respectful. P. A. R. And you'd do well to keep a mind to all three. I don't know who all is going to be up there with Mr. Pelton, but it sure as heck ain't going to be a bunch of steamer tramps."

I nod and glance down from the grandstand.

Beyond the hundreds, maybe thousands, of people pushing against the fence below us, the racetrack spreads out. It's so huge that it's impossible to take it all in at once. A nine-furlong dirt track surrounds a turf oval with eight jumps, each of which is capped with pink and white flowers. The perfectly groomed infield has a pond with two swans and a slew of ducks. The infield is smattered with track workers, mostly folks like me who don't have a nickel for each fist. Men stand near the finish line, pressed against the rail, scurrying back and forth, afraid they might miss a second of the excitement. If it's possible to be peaceful and bustling at the same time, it happens right here at Saratoga.

Mr. Hodge clucks at me like he does when we exercise horses. I follow him, and it feels as though I'm headed for the chopping block.

Mr. Pelton's box is on the front rail, about twenty feet above ground level and twenty feet before the wire. Short of being on horseback, it's the perfect spot to see a race. The boxes are no larger than closets and lined up one after the other. They each hold six tightly packed seats and are open to the boxes on either side, separated only by a white thigh-high wall. Men in jackets and women in dresses and peacock-feather hats squeeze into them, champagne flutes in hand. Even though the clubhouse is wide open to the outside, the air hangs thick with cigar smoke and expensive perfume. I glance around and notice how many boxes there actually are. Rows and rows of them climb up and back toward the con-course, where even more people are hanging over the railings.

And every one of them is here to spend money. Thousands of them. If there's a depression going on, it sure hasn't touched this part of Saratoga Springs.

"Jack." Mr. Pelton has a deep, lowing cow sort of voice. His broad body alone practically fills the box. His bushy white mustache curls up on the ends, and there's a redness in his cheeks that hints at a morning of exercising his elbow. He waves me over and turns his attention back to the track.

The mounts parade in a line from the paddock to the brand-new starting gate. Word around the backstretch is that the massive metal thing was shipped in pieces from down-state, assembled at the train station, and dragged here by a team of draft horses. It's the first time a gate's being used here in Saratoga. All the jockeys and all the horses have been busy training with them in preparation for today. Mr. Hodge says I'm as good a rider as he's ever seen in one.

"Have a seat, young man," Mr. Pelton says. "My wife is in the powder room. She won't be back for a few minutes. You know how women are."

I'm frozen. A rabbit in the eyes of a hungry snake. My brain knows I should obey, that I should do exactly as Mr. Pelton asks, but sitting in a box with him seems like something I shouldn't do.

"I asked you to take a seat," he says, this time more firmly.

Mr. Hodge pats me on the shoulder to urge me to do it. I squeeze into the box and slide my chair as far from Mr. Pelton as I can. My shoulder bumps into a girl sitting in the next box. She's wearing a white dress and a floppy straw hat. If it weren't for her stiff posture, which makes her look as though someone strapped a broomstick to her back, I'd say she looks about my age.

"Excuse me, miss," I say.

She glares at me as though I've disturbed her evening prayers. The girl is wearing long white gloves bunched up around her wrists to expose smooth, alabaster skin. She is gazing through a pair of opera glasses mounted on the end of a slender stick. Her head is craned to the side, and I realize she's not admiring the horses. She's staring across me at the bookmakers who are milling around the east end of the grandstand. She pulls out a small black notebook with gilded edges and scribbles down some notes.

Mr. Hodge removes his hat and presses it to his chest. "You'll have to excuse me, sir," he says to Mr. Pelton. "We have a horse running down there in the first."

"By all means, Gil," he says. "It's the boy with whom I need to speak."

My throat knots up, but I realize that if Mr. Pelton wants to toss me over the rail like yesterday's garbage, there's nothing I'd be able to do about it. Strangely, that settles me down. It's easier if everything is in someone else's hands.

Mr. Pelton rattles his racing form and looks over the early morning odds for the first race. "Who do you like in this one, Jack?"

I look at the Thoroughbreds being led onto the track. Each one prances alongside its lead pony, tossing its head and bucking. To most people, all Thoroughbreds look alike. And it's no wonder considering every one of the breed is descended from the same three horses: Byerly Turk, Darley Arabian, and Godolphin Arabian. To me, though, every horse looks different. Leg length. Muscle tone. Chest width. Coat shine. Face shape. Temperament. How it moves. Even the gleam in its eye. To me, every horse looks different like, when you look closely, every snowflake looks different.

Showboat is high atop Grand Slam. He is wearing purple and white silks, the colors of Pelton Stables. Grand Slam gives a little nervous buck. I know the smart thing would be to tell my boss that his own horse is looking good—that Grand Slam is a surefire winner—but I can't. Grand Slam has no chance. He's been running quirky ever since he nicked a hoof back at Belmont.

Then I see the number six. Sleek and dark, it strides past like there aren't thousands of screaming spectators hanging over the rails. Its ears are pricked and its hindquarters dappled. This horse is alert but calm. Calm and determined. I know a winning pony when I see one, and this here is a winning pony. This horse wants to win. The jockey is wearing blue and green silks, the colors of Bluewillow Stables. Bluewillow was in the next barn down from us in Belmont, but I've never seen that horse before.

"Who's the number six?" I ask.

Mr. Pelton peers down his nose at the racing form. "His name is Diablo Rose. Herb August purchased him from Argentina last year. It's his first race here in the States, but the horse performed reasonably well in South America. Do you have a feeling about him?"

"He's a nice one," I say.

Mr. Pelton looks through his binoculars at the bookies. "He's going off at twenty to one," he says. "You're sure about him?"

"The only sure thing is that horses are unpredictable," I say. "I'm just saying he looks nice."

Mr. Pelton strokes his mustache a few times and lifts his hand. A man in a white jacket comes, and Mr. Pelton hands him a bill. "Take this down to Long Tom Shaw," he says. "Put the full hundred on Diablo Rose to win."

"Wait. Wait a second here," I say through my panic. "I didn't even read the sheets today. I don't know the first thing about that horse."

"Then I suppose you'll lose me a hundred dollars."

"But—"

"Jack, if there is one thing I've learned as an owner, it's that folks in the stretch know a whole lot about horses. Today, I've decided to trust you."

Trust me? Today he's decided to trust me? Is this about Jasper after all?

"Mr. Pelton, I—"

He lifts a finger to me and drains his champagne glass. "Best thing they did was repeal that blasted Prohibition." He places his glass on the rail and refills it. White bubbles surge to the top, then sink back down. "Would you care for some bubbly?" he asks. "We can drink to Diablo Rose coming in at twenty to one."

"I don't think my stomach can handle a hundred-dollar bet. Maybe I'll have one if he wins."

A voice comes from over my shoulder. "You may as well have one now then." My head snaps around. It's the girl in the white dress. "Diablo Rose *is* going to win."

Mr. Pelton chuckles. "And who might you be, young lady?"

"Elizabeth Reed," she says. She extends her gloved hand across me like I'm not even there. Mr. Pelton takes it in his meaty paw.

"You must be Jim Reed's girl," Mr. Pelton says. "How old are you now, young lady? You must be fifteen? Sixteen?"

"Sixteen, sir."

"Sixteen, huh? Well dip my mustache in milk and lay me down in a kitchen full of kittens." Mr. Pelton leans back in his chair. It creaks under him. "I remember when you used to run around these boxes like a mouse in a maze. My, you've grown into a lovely young lady."

I'm not sure what Elizabeth looked like when she was younger, but there's no doubt she's a lovely young lady now. Even through all the lipstick and rouge and all that other junk girls cake on their faces, I can tell Elizabeth's got that beauty you see in a foal descended from good stock. She's got long blond hair that twists into tiny ringlets as thick as my thumb, and her pale skin covers delicate, high cheekbones.

A tiny smile curls up on one side of Elizabeth's face as if she wants to accept the compliment but is too modest to do so. Her eyes—her large hazel eyes—lower to her racing form.

"What about your father's horse?" Mr. Pelton asks. "Isn't Alabama Cyclone running in this one?"

"She's the number eight. Daddy thinks she's going to win, but he's sorely mistaken."

"Your father knows horses," Mr. Pelton says. "He's been racing them nigh on twenty years."

"Trust me. That mare of his is not Saratoga caliber."

Another girl, this one wearing a yellow dress and black gloves, makes her way through the clusters of people who fill the aisles. Her hat is tilted so much that it covers most of her face. Even though the crowd is near deafening, the girl takes the trouble to whisper into Elizabeth's ear. Elizabeth scribbles something down on a slip of paper and hands it to the girl, who saunters away.

"Miss Reed," Mr. Pelton says, leaning across me. "I want you to meet Jack Walsh. He's an up-and-coming jockey in my stable."

I stick out my hand to shake.

She gets a pinchy look on her face, like someone forgot to put the sugar in her lemonade. "Oh, an exercise boy," she says. "How nice to meet you."

When she doesn't offer her hand in return, it reminds me how I don't belong up here in the clubhouse. I belong in the picnic area or, better yet, in my stall on the backstretch. I sink lower into my seat and stare at the track. The starters begin to load the horses into the gate one by one.

Mr. Pelton leans into me so close I can smell his aftershave mixed with the booze on his breath. "I expect you're curious as to why I had you come up here," he says.

I don't say anything.

"I got word a few minutes ago about something that concerns me."

"Mr. Pelton, I can explain—"

"No need to explain," he says. "I understand completely."

"You do?"

He nods. "You haven't seen your father in over three years. It's only natural you'd want to see him."

I have no idea what he's talking about. Does Mr. Pelton think Jasper is my father?

"He telephoned my office this morning and gave word he'll be arriving in Saratoga tomorrow. He'll be on the eleven fifteen train."

I feel like a pregnant mare just took her hooves off my chest. This isn't about Jasper at all.

"He said he has some matters of importance to discuss with you."

What could my father need to speak with me about that he couldn't say over the telephone? Or by letter? Did something terrible happen? Would Mom be coming with him? Would Penny?

Mr. Pelton leans even closer, until I feel like he's breathing the air straight out of my lungs. The smell of aftershave and booze gets near overpowering. "Now, son, let me be clear. I don't want to hear any nonsense about you leaving with him. I have quite a bit invested in you."

"I don't think my father would ask me to leave."

Mr. Pelton lifts his hand to silence me. "These are tough times, and you're coming of age, Jack. If your father feels the screws tightening, he may want you back at the farm so he can jump into the workforce. I can't let that happen. I took you in when you were doing the local circuit with that lowlife . . . What was his name again?"

Just saying his name makes me want to curl up in a ball. "Tweed," I say.

"That's right, Tweed McGowan. And look at you now. You're my best exercise boy. You had better not leave me at the altar with a wedding ring in my hands. Are we clear?"

"Mr. Pelton, I'm not going anywhere. I've wanted to be a jockey my whole life. This is the best chance I've got."

"It's the only chance you've got." Mr. Pelton pours himself another glass of champagne. The bubbles rise to the lip of the glass, then run down the sides. He dabs at the wet railing with a napkin. "If you leave, I'll make sure no other stable hires you as long as you live."

Showboat's jacket pulls across my chest as if Niles, the
horse groom, threw a saddle on me and cinched it three
notches too tight. I want nothing more than to get up and
leave, to let things go back to the way they were when I woke
up this morning:

No Jasper.

No picking horses.

No sitting in a hot and sweaty box with Mr. Pelton.

"Business is business," Mr. Pelton says. His eyes lock onto
mine. "I want to make certain we're clear on this."

I give him a single nod.

"Excellent." Mr. Pelton breaks into a smile. "Now, enough
with the unpleasantries. It's opening day. Why don't you enjoy
the first race from here, son?"

I feel like a goldfish at the bottom of the bowl with
nowhere to go but into the net. "If it's all the same to you, sir,
I'd prefer to watch this one trackside. I want to see the action
on that new starting gate."

Mr. Pelton lifts his glass. "Then here's to Diablo Rose coming in on the nose." He takes a sip and slides his chair aside so
I can get past him.

"Why would you ever want to watch a race trackside?"
Elizabeth asks without taking her eyes from her opera glasses.
She's peering at the bookmakers again. "Those benches look
awfully uncomfortable. Are you too short to see over the railings from up here?"

"I'm sorry," I say. "Do you have a problem with me?"

She smiles a dismissive smile. "Just having a little fun."

"Well, save it for someone who cares," I mutter. I squeeze
my way out of the box. "Anyhow, a girl who won't return a simple handshake is lower than a worm in a posthole."

"How dare you!" A scowl flares up on Elizabeth's face and she rises. She's easily six inches taller than I am. Maybe more. Five minutes ago I was worried about Mr. Pelton tossing me over the railing. Now I'm concerned about Elizabeth. I stand as tall as I can without rising to my toes, but I barely make it up to her collarbone. I find myself taking the smallest step back.

"Watch your mouth," she says, "or I'll squash *you* like a worm."

I can't back down now, not from a girl, not with everyone watching. "Right," I say, "and Al Capone is going to be the next pope."

One of the ushers appears out of nowhere and places a firm hand on my shoulder. "Excuse me, Miss Reed," he says to Elizabeth. "Is there a problem?"

"No, no problem at all, Clyde. This swellhead was just leaving."

And she's right. I can't get out of there fast enough. I rush along the aisle and down the stairs to ground level. Down here the track is packed with everyday people. Going from top hats to tweed caps, from champagne glasses to Hedrick beer bottles, makes me feel closer to normal. Finally I can breathe again.

And I need to breathe. I need to clear my head so I can think on why my father is coming to Saratoga tomorrow, so I can figure out how to get rid of Jasper, so I can fume about that stiff-backed Elizabeth Reed. Boy, do I need to fume about her!

But it's the first race of opening day.

It's the first time they're using that sparkling new starting gate.

It's time to watch some horses.

5

Near the finish line, hundreds of racing fans press against the rail, take up every free inch of space. As soon as a spot opens, another body is there to fill it. That's fine by me. It leaves more room at the starting gate, which is where I'd rather be. There's something about seeing the jockeys dressed in their flashy silk jackets high atop their even flashier mounts. I like to see up close how those horses take off—how their hooves scoop yard-long trenches in the dirt as they explode forward. I like to see the jockeys clutch to their horses' manes so as not to tug the reins back or have their saddles lurch right out from under them.

And I like to see ten horses become a race.

The trouble with watching from the starting line is all the walking. Since every race ends in the same spot, each one starts someplace different. This race is ten furlongs. Saratoga has a nine-furlong track, so the gate is to the left of the finish line a ways. The horses do a full lap and then some—a mile and a quarter.

It's hot out—that steamy kind of hot that makes your clothes stick to your skin. The stench of sweat mixes with turned earth. Popcorn bags and discarded newspapers litter the ground. People chatter back and forth about the horses and the weather and the numbers. Always the numbers. Odds and percentages and payouts and dollar amounts. I feel right at home.

I squeeze between two stocky men and poke my nose over the rail. Showboat sits atop Grand Slam, and I imagine myself up there in those purple and white silks parading around for everyone to see. Grand Slam seems jittery—not just excited but nervous—probably from all the travel, the thrill of opening day, and seeing that narrow chute in front of his nose. He never took to the starting gate like the other horses in our stable. As they approach, Showboat tries to calm his mount by patting him on the side of the neck. I want to call out to him, to tell Showboat that Grand Slam likes it when you whisper in his ear.

But what's the point? Showboat can't hear me from way over here—not with the crowd chattering as loud as it is.

A skittish Grand Slam tries to back out of the chute, but a track worker shoves him hard from behind. The horse whinnies and rears up.

A loud clang rings out as Showboat's head smashes into the support bar. I know it's twenty yards away and I know the crowd is making all sorts of a ruckus, but I swear I can hear the snapping sound from here. Showboat drops to the ground like a crate of apples bouncing off the back of a truck. Someone screams. The crowd gasps and then falls silent. A worker drags Showboat's limp figure out from under Grand Slam's stomping hooves and leaves him lying in the dirt. The starting crew clusters around him. Men shout into the crowd for a doctor.

Spectators push forward to get a better look. Shoulders, elbows, hips crush me against the rail. I try to climb over, but there are too many people pressing forward. I can't get my leg up. Crawling under would mean pushing through a thick row of thorny hedges.

"Help!" I call to the people standing around. "Help me over!"

"Stay put," one of them says. "You're no doctor."

"I'm Showboat's apprentice," I say. "I ride with Pelton Stables."

Unseen hands cup me under the arms and boost me up. I swing my leg over the rail and toss my body to the other side. I land hard in the dirt and spring to my feet. By the time I get to Showboat, more people have gathered around. His helmet lies on his chest in tattered pieces. Most jockeys cut the lining and much of the shell out to lighten weight; Showboat's helmet is no different. It's a crumpled mass of wet cardboard covered in torn purple silk.

Showboat's face is bright red, and his mouth is stretched so tight I can count his teeth back to the third molars. His eyes swivel toward me.

"Hey, Jack," Showboat manages to say.

I kneel at his side. He's panting in short, quick bursts. He tries to swallow but instead lets out a low wail. A small trickle of blood runs from his forehead and disappears into his dark hair, which lies flat and wet against his skull.

"I'm here." I reach out to grab his forearm, but then think better of it. If I move him, I might hurt him worse. But it's more than that. I feel as though if I touch him it will make this whole situation real. It could have just as easily been me on that horse.

"You gotta help me get back up on old Grand Slam there," he says. "He's gonna win this one. I can feel it."

"Slam's a good horse," I say. "He's a damn good horse."

Showboat smiles so big his eyes squint up and press out a couple of tears. "I gotta ride, Jack. I just gotta." I can barely hear him through the commotion of the crowd and the rushing in my ears, but he goes on. "Sara's due next month. I gotta win purses for the baby. I gotta win purses for the baby." His face is pointing straight up, and I realize that nothing is moving below his jaw. The toes of his boots point at odd angles, like his left is at eleven o'clock and his right is all the way at three.

"Let's just wait for the doctor," I say. "And Mr. Hodge'll be here soon. He'll know what to do."

"Stop your crying," Showboat says, and it's the first time I realize that I am. I drag a sleeve across my nose and sniffle back the tears.

Showboat tries to lift his head, but he only manages a grunt. "I never meant nothing by what I told Hodge about you," he says. "All that guff about you having a bum shoulder."

"Sure, Showboat, I know."

He tries to nod back at me, but instead he lets loose a whine. "Hey, is that my jacket you got on?"

I look down at it. Mud and snot cover the left lapel and sleeve. The seam across the shoulder is torn. I must've caught it on something as I hopped over the rail. This jacket is a wreck. "Mr. Hodge told me I could borrow it," I say. "I promise I'll get it cleaned up nice for you."

"Don't sweat it," Showboat says. He grunts again, this time louder. "Just give it on back. I'm getting awful cold."

6

WHEN I GET BACK TO THE BARN, I'M NUMB. THE guys are playing cards on a bunch of crates they've stacked up. Fireside stands in his stall, his rectangular, charcoal head sloping down over the door so he can get at his hay and salt lick, which are hanging in baskets low to the ground. Spoons the monkey is curled up on a crate under the shed awning. He's taken off his jacket and is using it as a pillow. Niles and another groom are washing down one of the other horses in the shade of a huge elm. I'm the only one here who knows about Showboat, and once I break the news I'm going to smudge this perfect painting.

"Jack!" Bucky hollers as soon as he catches sight of me. The boys drop their cards and scramble around as if they're starving ponies and I've got sugar cubes.

"So what happened?" Oatmeal asks.

"Mr. Pelton asked you to ride, right?" Pug adds.

I shake my head slow. I place Showboat's jacket next to Spoons, who scampers up into the rafters with an apple tucked in the crook of an arm. I strip off my shirt. It's smeared with blood, but the guys are so hungry for me to talk that they don't notice. I toss the jacket to the ground near my stall door. "He just heard from my dad is all."

Their eyes drop to the floor. We don't talk much about family or home around here. It grinds salt into wounds we'd rather leave scabbed over. Oatmeal scoops up his cards and slides them into his pocket. Pug and Bucky sit back down.

I want to tell them about Showboat, but I can't find the words.

"Hey, you know a lot about racing, Jack," Bucky says to me, his keys jingling on his belt as he shifts on his crate to face me. "What is the highest number of starting horses ever?"

"Huh?" I splash my face at the rain barrel. It feels like someone else is holding the reins to my brain and I'm just going through the motions.

"We have a little bet going, the guys and me," Bucky says. "We're betting on the highest number of starters in any race."

"You know," Oatmeal adds. "What race had the most horses in it?"

"Sixty-six," I mumble. "It was the 1929 Grand National Steeplechase."

"I told you!" Bucky cries out. "I read that one in the sports pages a few years back."

"You don't read," Pug says.

"All right, I heard some guys talking about it."

Fireside snorts. He shifts uneasily, and his head twitches around. I wonder if he can smell the blood on my shirt.

"Showboat got hurt," I say. "He got hurt bad."

All three of the guys stare at me, and it takes a few seconds for me to realize they're waiting for more. Once I start talking, the words dump out like water from a kicked-over trough. I tell them how Grand Slam reared up and how Showboat's skull smashed into the overhead rail. I tell them about the awful snapping noise and how the ambulance took more than a half hour to get there. I tell them how Showboat couldn't move his arms or legs and how he said they felt like they were on fire. I tell them about how the starters fashioned a makeshift stretcher from a ladder and a few jackets to pull Showboat to the side so the race could go off anyway. I didn't see the finish, but Mr. Pelton made sure to clap me on the back and tell me how I won him two grand. I was too upset to care. The only part I don't mention is how Showboat was sobbing about his wife and new baby and how he isn't going to be able to earn the dough to feed them.

By the time I finish, the boys look as numb as I feel. The sounds of the track go on like nothing happened. Grooms holler back and forth as they hot-walk the horses. Pickup trucks and hay haulers rattle along the rutted dirt paths between the sheds. A trainer and a freelance jockey struggle with a young colt. The idea that things are going on as usual makes me want to punch a splintery wall. How can people enjoy a day at the races knowing Showboat may never ride again?

Bucky jumps to his feet and rushes on over to me.

Startled, Spoons scampers down a post and leaps onto the edge of Fireside's door. He hops into my arms and curls up like when he was a baby. His dark face turns this way and that, taking it all in. He hisses at Bucky.

"You've got to lose weight, Jack," Bucky says. He pokes at my belly like he's some kind of doctor. "It's awful what happened to Showboat and all, but one man's trash is another man's treasure."

"What the hell's that supposed to mean?" Oatmeal says. "Showboat ain't trash. He's a good rider."

"Are you a retard?" Pug says. "Bucky means that Jack is gonna probably ride in Showboat's place."

Thinking about taking over for Showboat makes my guts thrash like a nervous colt's tail. It could have just as easily been me on Grand Slam's back. I exercised him twice last week. It was me who helped gate-train him.

"You want me to look for a payday on account of Showboat's accident?" I say to Bucky. "I don't want any part of that."

"Don't look at it that way," Bucky says. He starts pacing between the awning posts. "Someone's going to have to ride Pelton's horses." He taps me square in the chest a bunch of times, and Spoons scrambles to my shoulder. "That's you, Jack. There ain't no one else. You have to cut weight. You have to cut weight fast."

Pug picks up a stack of horse blankets and tosses them to me. "Wrap yourself up in these. We'll get you doing calisthenics," he says.

I toss the blankets back at him. "You guys are acting like Showboat's dead. He'll be fine. That guy's as tough as a new riding crop." Even as the words pass my lips, I know I'm hanging on to a fairy tale. Showboat will be lucky to pick up his brand-new baby or hug his wife. Hell, he'll be lucky to take a leak by himself ever again.

Oatmeal stands up and pounds his fist into his open palm. "Bucky's right," he says. "Mr. Hodge will be in here before you know it to drop the buzz."

"They're right." The voice is familiar, and my shoulders hunch up.

Elizabeth Reed.

How long could she have been listening?

All our heads swivel around, and there she is, clutching her black book to her chest. Her hat is pulled low over her eyes. With the sunlight behind her, I can see the shape of her long body through her dress. My face gets hot and my eyes flick to Fireside, who still seems twitchy. Sometimes I think that horse and me share the same thoughts.

Maybe manners aren't something the other guys were born with, or maybe they just forgot them after being on the backstretch so long. Either way, Bucky, Oatmeal, and Pug do nothing to hide that they're staring at her.

"What are you doing down here?" I say.

"See, I was right," Oatmeal says. "There *was* a princess who threw her kerchief to Jack!"

The other guys laugh.

"Shut up," I tell them. "She's the daughter of some fat cat from the boxes and she was just leaving."

Elizabeth plants a fist on her hip. "My father is *not* a fat cat."

Spoons squeaks and leaps from my shoulder into the darkness of Fireside's stall.

"Oh yeah?" I say. "What would you call him?"

"My father works harder in one day than any of you swellheads will work your whole lives."

"Doubt that," Pug mutters. "If your father's got a box in Saratoga, then he's a fat cat."

I nod. "If he can afford to bring his whole family to the races for a month," I say, "he's a fat cat."

Elizabeth folds her arms and spins around. "I won't stand here and get razzed by four exercise boys." She says "exercise boys" like she's spitting the words into the dirt. "Even if one of them is about to be promoted to apprentice."

With that, she breezes off around the corner of the barn.

The guys and I exchange glances.

"Promoted?" Bucky says.

"Could she know for sure?" Oatmeal adds.

I chase after her with the boys not far behind. "What are you talking about?" I ask. "Who's getting promoted?"

"Never you mind," Elizabeth says without slowing her pace. I'm amazed how well she walks in the dirt wearing high-heeled shoes. "If I wanted to take crap from you, I'd stand near the manure wagon while you muck the stalls."

I grab Elizabeth's arm. I pull her to a stop and spin her around. I know it's not proper for me to handle a girl like that, but we aren't in the clubhouse anymore. We aren't in her fat-cat father's fancy box. We're on the backstretch. The rules are different here.

Elizabeth glares at me.

"Tell me," I say. "What did you hear?"

She shakes her head. "Apologize first."

"Apologize for what?"

"For calling my father a fat cat."

"I didn't mean nothing by it."

"Then it won't be so hard for you to apologize."

"Go on," Bucky says from behind one of the awning posts. "Tell her you're sorry."

No one around here takes back something he said. It's a sign of being soft. But I need to know what Elizabeth overheard more than anything. So the words that hardly ever pass my lips pass my lips: "I'm, um . . . I'm sorry."

Elizabeth's mouth turns up slightly at the edges. When she smiles, a wrinkle works its way into her forehead that I might have thought was cute if it weren't attached to her face. "Sorry for what?" she asks. "And speak up. I couldn't hear you so well the first time."

She's going to ride this one hard.

"Sorry for calling your father a fat cat," I say, this time louder.

Elizabeth considers my words and then finally comes out with it. "Okay," she says in a near whisper. "I heard Mr. Pelton talking to his wife as soon as they pulled Showboat out from under the starting gate. He's going to want you to ride tomorrow."

"Tomorrow?" I say. "We don't have any ponies on the card for tomorrow."

"Wednesday then, you ox-headed midget!"

The other exercise boys burst into laughter. Even Spoons, whose head is poking out of Fireside's stall, screeches in delight. "Ox-headed midget!" Pug says as he teeters on the rim of a water trough.

"Shut your yap!" Oatmeal shoves Pug, and he loses his balance. Pug lands heavy on the packed dirt. "Let Jack talk to the gal."

"You horse's ass," Pug says, rubbing his side. He stands, and the three exercise boys come out from the shadow of the barn.

"How much do you weigh?" Elizabeth asks, looking me over like I'm a roast she's thinking on buying at the butcher shop.

"Around one sixteen."

"No, no, no." She shakes her head like she's trying to send her hat flying off. "With the imposts your horses are likely to get, you're way too heavy. With your bug boy allowance, you're going to have to cut about ten pounds."

An impost is the amount of weight the track officials figure a horse has to carry in a race. The better the horse, the greater the impost. World-class horses carry around one thirty, while slower horses carry as little as a hundred. The idea is to even out the odds a little. To account for how green apprentices are, bug boys are allowed to carry five pounds less until their fortieth win or their one-year racing anniversary.

Elizabeth is right. Even with my five-pound allowance, after I add my saddle, boots, and silks, I'll come in over the mark. The mounts I have a chance of getting will have a much lighter impost—one hundred ten at the most.

"Ten pounds in two days?" Bucky says. "Not a problem."

The nibble of egg sandwich I had with Jasper not two hours earlier seems to swell up in my stomach. "What do you know about cutting weight?" I ask Bucky. "You're a hundred and eight no matter how much you stuff in your face."

"Jockeys around here drop weight all the time," Bucky says. "Ten pounds in two days is duck soup."

"If I'm going to cut ten pounds in two days, you're going to have to stop talking about soup."

He gives me a thumbs-up and one of his snaggletoothed grins.

I look Elizabeth over. Standing there in her big hat and white gloves, she looks like every other debutante that fills the grandstands. But she spouted off those impost figures like

it was second nature. "How do you know so much about racing?" I ask her.

"I have to know it."

"Why?"

"I just do." She looks down at the clumps of weeds poking
through the dirt.

"Because your father owns all those horses?"

She takes a few seconds to look me over and then holds out
her journal. I take it, run my finger over the gilded edges, and
open the black leather cover. The pages are lined with
columns, like an accountant's ledger. Each column is penciled
tight with dates, odds, and other racing figures. There are sta-
tistics and results from Belmont, Aqueduct, Pimlico, and
Hialeah.

"What are you, some kind of mathematics whiz or something?"

I look at her, hoping she might fill me in, and for the first
time her intense eyes—eyes that could pierce the thick steel
of a bank vault as if it were straw—lock on mine.

"You're looking at the only female bookie in the racing
world."

7

ELIZABETH FANS HERSELF WITH HER PROGRAM AS WE make our way along the backstretch. Most of the owners' barns are across the road from the main track near the Oklahoma Training Track, but Mr. Pelton's been bringing horses to Saratoga so long he gets first choice. Our sheds are right behind the flat track, the one we race on, and it's only a short walk to the premier spot to watch horses in upstate New York.

Most fans would be full of oohs and aahs back here—all the famous horses and jockeys crawling all over the place— but not Elizabeth. Elizabeth doesn't turn her head—not even once.

"I don't have a bankroll like the big bookies, so I have to cut the odds a little," she says. "Even so, they're better numbers than you'd get with any of those small-timers trolling the stands."

Bucky, Oatmeal, and Pug agreed to finish whatever work was left at the barn and to blow out my horses for the next

few days as long as I started working at cutting weight. I
know walking the backstretch with a girl isn't really cutting
weight, but I need to show Elizabeth at least a little hospital-
ity for coming all the way down here to tell me the news. Anyhow, we *are* walking. That has to count for something.

"Why would anyone bet with you if they could go down to
the real bookies and place a wager on their own? You said
yourself they'd get better odds."

She looks at me as though I have six eyes and two noses.
"It might be true that this season is the first in twenty-seven
that bookmakers can operate openly at the track, but women
still aren't allowed to wager down there in the betting circle."

"They're not?"

She shakes her head. Her blond ringlets bounce like each
has got a life of its own. "The men are getting a hundred to
one down there, but the women have to take action with the
shady small-timers at fifteen to one. So, I decided to go into
business and split the difference. On a bet like that, I'd give
something like forty to one."

"What if the small-timers catch on?" I say. "You can't just
go up and down the aisles hawking your odds like some kind
of fishmonger."

"Of course not," she says. "Those goons are vicious, terri-
torial. They'd find a way to put me out of business. And I've
got no interest in getting knocked around by a bunch of
creeps some night outside the Union Hotel."

"So what's your secret?"

She looks me over, like she's sizing me up. "I have a very
exclusive clientele," she says. "I only take bets from young
women—in particular, ones whom I know. I keep it small.
Sometimes I'll get a new account by word of mouth, but I re-

strict betting to five or ten dollars per race until I get to know her. It helps me limit my exposure."

Elizabeth saying that word, "exposure," gets my brain thinking about seeing more of her arms, more of her legs, more of everything. "Exposure to what?" I say.

"To risk, of course. If I take on a bet I'm not able to cover, I can't rightly go running to my father to help me out. He thinks betting is a man's game—that women have no head for numbers. He'd send me straight back home to New York City—probably lock me in a convent and toss the key into the deepest part of the Hudson River."

Even though I've only known Elizabeth for a short time, the thought of this sassy girl in a convent borders on comical. "Come on," I say. "He must know you're doing this."

"Daddy has no idea. That's why I have Jane. She's my runner."

"Runner?"

I feel like a dunce. I have no idea what a runner is. Even though I've been around racetracks for years, I've never gotten involved with betting. Unlike most track workers, who gamble and drink their paychecks away, then spend anything left with one of the dames at the brothel down on Caroline Street, I send every nickel home to my folks. I figure if I work hard at learning what it is I've got to learn, I just might go around the carousel a few times in this business. And that's the only way I'll have a chance to get my hands on that brass ring.

"You mean the girl who came around in the yellow dress?" I say. "The one who whispered in your ear?"

Elizabeth nods, and her blond ringlets do a different dance, just as mesmerizing as the first. "Every good bookie needs a runner," she says. "Jane works the crowd. She knows which girls I deal with and which ones are off limits. Between races, she visits their boxes. They tell her what horses they like, and I write out the slip. In exchange, I cut Jane in for ten percent."

It makes sense. It makes perfect sense.

"Strikes me as funny," she says.

"What does?"

"Our fathers think we're just a bunch of dumb girls gossiping back and forth about boys. Heck, Jane and I are doing more work than any of those men. I rather like the irony of it all."

"You must be swimming in cash," I say.

She seems to clutch her book tighter. "A business like this, you've got to expect swings."

There's something exciting about Elizabeth running her game under everyone's noses, but I think a girl—even one as sharp as she is—would be in way over her head if the other bookies found out. Bookmaking is a rough game.

She reaches up and fiddles with a gold locket hanging on a chain around her neck. My eyes follow her hand, then stray down to study her curves against the flimsy material of her dress. She smiles and asks, "What are you looking at?"

My cheeks flush. "I like your necklace."

The bell for the third race sounds. The horses break from the starting gate and gallop toward us. It's an eight-furlong—or one-mile—race, which means those ponies have to go at a pretty good clip. The nine Thoroughbreds are in a tight pack as they clear the first turn and head past us into the back-stretch.

Even though I ride every day, it still amazes me to see a

one-hundred-and-ten-pound jockey balanced atop an eleven-hundred-pound animal sailing along at forty miles an hour. Both jockey and horse move as one in a rhythm that—just by watching—I can feel in my bones. The pounding of hooves sends a cloud of dust around us. I fill my chest with the rich smell.

"Don't you have to be back for the end of the race?" I ask her. "You know, to pay out or something?"

"It would be unseemly for us to pass money back and forth," she says. "All my girls have running accounts. Anyhow, Jane can take care of anything that comes up. She's a whip."

"It sounds to me like you've got all the angles covered."

She smiles. "Almost."

We stop talking to watch the horses enter the far turn. With so many track workers packed into the infield, only the horses' heads and the jockeys' bright silk helmets bob into view. As the race enters the final stretch, a few Thoroughbreds begin nosing ahead of the pack. The crowd comes alive. I can't see who's in the lead, but it has to be close. The noise doubles with every stride, and the spectators are on their feet.

"So what do you think about getting promoted?" Elizabeth asks. She turns around and leans against the rail, her back to the race. She lets the sun soak into her shoulders.

I point to the finish line. "Don't you care who wins?"

"It doesn't matter," she says. "I have all my bets covered. No matter what, I make money."

"But the racing, it's all so exciting."

"For you it's exciting. For me it's business."

My jaw squeezes tight. I get up every morning before sunrise to exercise ponies. I spend a good chunk of the day chest-deep in filth mucking stalls. I do all the chores around the barn, hot-walk horses, make sure all the animals are taken care of. Every day, I risk getting hurt. Getting hurt bad. Like Showboat. And I do it all for a measly five bucks a week. This girl has a racket going. She can stand here with her back to the race. No matter who wins she makes money. And no matter what she thinks, her father will always be there to bail her out.

And that's the difference between her and me.

"So, what do you think about getting promoted?" she says again. The wind blows a lock of hair across her face. She brushes it aside with her finger. "You must be shaking in your silks."

"I don't think it's sunk in yet."

"Well, it better sink in soon."

"I won't start dropping weight until I get word from Mr. Hodge," I say.

"That seems so . . . I don't know." She waves her black book in the air as she searches for the word. "It seems so fatalistic."

"Fatal what?"

"Fa-ta-lis-tic." She says each syllable like she's explaining it to a three-year-old. "You know, accepting things as if you have no control over them." Then she adds in a softer voice, "Like those freckles across your nose."

I don't miss that she's noticed my freckles, but I go on. "I *don't* have control," I say. "I don't have control over anything."

Elizabeth pushes off the rail and starts to walk away. Even though the temperature is somewhere in the nineties, I can feel her warmth as she goes past. "Straight-out pathetic," she says.

I trail after her. "*I'm* pathetic? You're the one who sits up there in that box of your father's peering down at the world through the safe end of a set of opera glasses."

Elizabeth spins to face me. Her cheeks are bright pink. "You don't know the first thing about me, so don't stand here and pretend you do. But I suppose it's easier that way, isn't it?"

"What's easier?"

"To resent me. You're about to face the biggest opportunity of your life, and you're sitting around waiting until it's a sure thing. Well, there aren't any sure things, Jack Walsh, not unless you make them that way."

I didn't expect her to snap like she did, and it feels like a punch in the gut. "It's more complicated than that," I say, the fight gone from my words.

"No," she says, looking me straight in the eyes. "It's not."

I know she's wrong, but she's also beautiful. Aside from horses, there aren't too many beautiful things in my life, and I want more than anything for Elizabeth to like me. Things are complicated. Things are more complicated than she can imagine, but I'm not going to tell her that. Not now, anyway.

Then I realize my mouth has been hanging open like a dopey horse's as it reaches for a carrot.

Elizabeth cracks a smile, and I look down at the dirt.

The truth is I've wanted to be a jockey ever since the first time my diaper hit the saddle. Now that it's staring me in the face, I'm terrified. I look over at the grandstands. There have to be ten thousand people here today. An average day draws about six. Thoroughbred racing is the biggest sport in America, maybe the world, and Saratoga is the biggest of the big time. Me having a chance to ride here is like a sandlot ballplayer having a chance to take the mound in the World Series.

"I don't know." Elizabeth tucks her book under her arm. "It seems to me you should be excited."

"It's aces," I say. "But I'm not doing any celebrating until the news comes from the big man. It's only ten pounds. How hard could it be?"

Her hazel eyes look me up and down. I want to get closer, to see how many colors are swimming in them. "I'm sorry if you're sorry," she says.

"What exactly are you sorry for?" I say it playfully. I want her to squirm like she made me squirm in front of the boys.

She smiles. "I'm sorry for snubbing you up there in the clubhouse on the condition that you're sorry for making all kinds of nasty assumptions about me."

I pretend to think on it for a few seconds. "Agreed," I say, extending my hand.

Elizabeth pulls off her satin glove one finger at a time until the whole length of it slips off at once.

We shake. Her hand is soft, like she's never done much more than push a pencil around a black ledger book her whole life. But I'm in the process of agreeing not to make assumptions about her, and that's an assumption. I push the thought from my mind.

Elizabeth sets her hat so the brim droops just above her eyes. "Well, if you're planning to do any celebrating, be sure to call me." She scribbles something on the corner of one of her ledger pages, tears it off, and hands it to me. It's a telephone number. "We're staying at the Adelphi."

"Hey," I say to her as she turns to walk off. "Not two hours ago you were looking down your nose at me and calling me a little exercise boy like it was the worst thing in the world."

A cloud of dust wraps around her as she spins to face me.

"That was when you were an exercise boy," she says, squinting against the sun. "You're a bug boy now. I like bug boys."

She spins again, and I stare at her walking away. As she heads back to the grandstands, I realize that, even wearing fancy high heels in the rutted dirt, Elizabeth still struts better than a world-class pacer.

8

I SHOVE TWO FINGERS DOWN MY THROAT AGAIN. A WAVE surges through my chest so hard it feels near like my ribs are going to crack. This time, all that comes out is a stringy goo that sears the back of my throat. I spit the slime into a bucket at the foot of my cot.

The Oracle confirmed what I already knew. I've got a lot of weight to lose. With my gear in hand, I weigh a hundred and sixteen pounds two ounces, and the Oracle doesn't lie. Jockeys call the scale "the Oracle" because their fates hang on the number it comes up with. If you're a few ounces too heavy, someone else rides in your place.

It's as simple as that.

Elizabeth was right too. After the tenth race, Mr. Hodge came down to the shed and told me I'd be riding starting Wednesday. He shook my hand like I was John D. Rockefeller and I'd just struck oil for the first time. The trouble is, now that my big chance is here, there's nothing I want less. From the moment Mr. Hodge broke the news, I had forty-six hours to drop the weight.

He told me I'll be riding Rusty Gate in the third race and Lucky Chance in the fifth. Even though I'm greener than a willow branch in springtime, if they were my horses I'd want me riding them too. I've worked both of them about a million times.

Rusty Gate is a strong mare and has been assigned a one-hundred-and-fifteen-pound impost. If she were my only mount, I'd have no problem. I'd only have to lose a few pounds. But Mr. Hodge wants me to ride Lucky Chance too. Lucky's got a pretty poor record and only has a one-hundred-and-six-pound impost in a low-stakes claiming race. That means I'll have to lose somewhere around ten pounds. That might be a walk in the park for a two-hundred-and-twenty-pound boxer. During a bout, a heavyweight sweats off a pound a round. For me, losing that kind of weight is scaling the Himalayas.

I wipe my face with a damp cloth and suck a few drops of water from it. I wonder how Showboat's doing down at the hospital, poor guy. I've asked a few people, but no one seems to have the inside track. Last I heard, they're bringing in a surgeon from Albany, but I don't trust those guys, with their bright lights and sharp silver tools. Seems to me they do more harm than good.

After all my puking and sleeping the night in Showboat's smelly rubber hot suit, I feel a little dizzy, but it's time to go meet my father down at the train station. I wrap a horse blanket around myself and begin the trot down Union Avenue. The sun rises higher, and the heat starts to weigh me down.

When I first started cutting weight, I felt hungry. I'm not
sure whether it was from not having any food or from knowing I wouldn't be eating a bite for the next two days. For a
while, I felt hungrier than I ever have in my life. Famished. I
wanted to eat grass, dirt, rocks—anything that would fill my
belly. After some laps around the track and few hours of calisthenics in the rubber suit, the hunger went away. What came
next was a strange tightness across my gut. At least the pain
was gone. It was tough getting to sleep, but I managed to pass
out for a few hours. Now, I just feel edgy, like everything
around me is clearer and closer. The breeze in the grass sounds
like a storm—like I can hear each blade rubbing on the ones
around it. A single footstep is an explosion in my head.

A taxicab slows and honks at me to see if I want to hop in,
but I wave him away. He wouldn't want my sweaty, shambling
self in his backseat anyway. I'm a dripping mess. I wind
around Congress Park, past Canfield Casino, and through
downtown Saratoga, where every person turns his or her head
to stare. I make my way up Broadway and turn left onto
Church Street. The station is only a few blocks from here.

The Saratoga train station is like dozens of others I've vis-
ited while I've bounced from one track to another. Five tracks
wide, the station gets a lot of use. It's the most popular way
for people to get here from downstate. The red brick of the
station house is bright and clean, but the pointy roof with its
rough shingles makes it seem older, like something out of the
nineteenth century. Cast-iron support beams make the platform a dense forest.

Even though the station's overhang offers plenty of shade,
I stand in the sun, to the side of the platform. I want to
melt—to sweat off as much weight as I can. My legs feel as

rubbery as my suit, but I shift from side to side in a light march. The hotter I can get the better. Sweat fills my shoes, and my feet squish with every step. Some jockeys can spit off a pound or more in a few hours, but I have nothing left. My mouth is a desert with no oasis. I lick my lips and taste only salt.

What will my father think when he steps off the train and sees me sweating Niagara Falls? Will he understand that this is my big chance? I figure he might, once he finds out how much money I can make as a bug boy. I get ten percent of the purse if I win, and purses run a thousand bucks or more. My cut from one race alone would be more than the farm makes in a month, and I can run four or five races in a day!

A woman on one of the benches stares at me like I might be a sideshow freak cast off from the three-ring circus that set up down by the recreation fields. I guess I do look pretty out of the ordinary with a heavy horse blanket wrapped around me in the dead middle of the summer. I feel giddy, so I bare my teeth at her and hiss like one of the feral cats that roam the orchards back home. Her glance slides to her shoes.

By the time the 11:15 pulls in, the platform is filled with people. Steam blasts from under the engine, and the porters start hauling trunks and suitcases and hatboxes on and off the coaches. People embrace their friends and relatives as they find one another. They rush to the black taxicabs lined up like rows of burnt buns. And everyone keeps a good distance from me.

It's been a long time since I've seen my father. I remember he's always clean-shaven and has short brown hair like mine. I remember his square jaw and how his teeth are just crooked enough for someone to notice. He has little lines around his dark eyes that crinkle up the same way whether he's angry or smiling. I figure those lines are probably deeper by now. After all, it's been more than three years. I think on the last time I saw him. It was the day he brought me into town to send me off with Tweed.

"Tweed McGowan is a good man," my father said as he straightened my bow tie. "He knows the horse business like nobody else."

My father said Tweed's name like we were lucky to know the guy, like his name should be up on a movie theater marquee. I wasn't sure if my father really was awed by Tweed or if he was just playing it up for my sake.

"I can't tell you how many youngsters he's brought into horse racing," my father said to me. "Some of them are big-time jockeys now, making loads and loads of money. You know what they say: Give a man a fish and he'll eat for a day . . ."

I finished it for him: "Teach a man to fish and he'll eat for a lifetime."

My father smiled right then. "That's right, Son. Tweed is going to teach you how to fish. I know how much you want to help out your old man—your whole family for that matter."

I pressed my lips together and nodded faster than a woodpecker so my father wouldn't see how close I was to crying. Then, I bent forward to adjust the zipper on my valise. As I knelt down, I pretended like I had an itch and wiped my eye on my shoulder. I did love riding, but I had never been away from the farm before—not even for a single night. From what my dad told me, Tweed and I would be leaving that afternoon to go out to Buffalo. From there we'd follow the amateur circuit through the Midwest. To me, Buffalo seemed like a different country. The Midwest, another world.

My father grabbed my shoulders. His eyes were just like Penny's. Even though my sister was always such a pest, I knew right then I'd miss her most of all. "Jack," he said to me. "Even though we're desperate for the extra money, you don't have to go. I want to make that clear."

I knew he was lying. I knew he couldn't feed all of us. Just the week before I'd overheard him talking to Ma about it. "Dire straits" were the words he'd used. When I saw Ma pouring water into the pea soup so we could stretch it a few more days, I made up my mind. I had to go. I had no choice.

"No, it's fine," I said. "I'm just a little scared."

"I'm scared too." He pulled me toward him for our last hug. "You'll be fine, kiddo. You're a fighter."

"I suppose."

Hell, back then I didn't know what scared was—I didn't know what terrified was—not until I was making the circuit with Tweed. I knew it wasn't my father's fault what was going on, but I also knew that if my dad—if our farm—brought in more money, I could've escaped and run home.

I shake away the memory and go back to sifting through the crowd with my eyes. Has my father grown a mustache? A beard? I don't see him anywhere. Did he walk right past me and I didn't recognize him? I look all around, but no one even resembles him. Every person that isn't him who steps off that train cinches the belt one notch tighter. I figured he'd be the first one off. I figured he'd stand by the door the whole ride and rush right out and scoop me up.

By the time the conductor blows his whistle, I know I'm not going to see my father—not today anyway. I wait until the platform is all but empty. The luggage is loaded and the train is ready for its journey farther north. The steam engine lets out a final hiss—like a long sigh—and begins to pull away.

I feel like throwing up, but there's nothing left to heave out.

I trot back toward the track. It's the longest two miles or so I can remember.

I head back through an alleyway between a theater and a hotel to avoid the long way around. When I dart out onto Broadway, the smell of car exhaust hits me. I trot past a market, several boutiques, and a druggist. A jewelry store and a haberdasher. Several more moving picture theaters. Music tumbles from each restaurant along Broadway, sounds mixing, terrible and beautiful at the same time. I don't turn my head once.

I kick a tin can in front of me and focus on the clattering it makes until it skitters under a fruit cart. The vendor glares, but after he gets a good look at me, his expression softens. He offers me an apple. It's an Idared—just like the kind we have out in the orchard back home. The thought of the tart pink flesh sends a shudder through my body. My stomach rages inside of me. I strain to keep my arms at my sides. I want to grab that apple and stuff it in my mouth. I want to eat everything on that cart.

But I can't. I have to make weight.

I shake my head and keep on trotting toward the track.

Somewhere in the distance, a whistle pierces the air. In my mind, I can see that train winding its way through the dense pine forest onward, north, into the Adirondack Mountains. A train that never had my father on it. Tears have to weigh something, so I figure my visit to the station wasn't a complete waste.

9

WHEN SPOONS CATCHES SIGHT OF ME ROUNDING the corner of the barn, he jumps up onto one of the horseshoe crates. It's an hour or so after his usual lunchtime, and he won't rest until he's got some food in his belly. He tugs at his jacket and scampers back and forth on the crates stacked along the side of the barn without taking his sad, hungry eyes off me. Oatmeal sees me coming too. He drops the can of saddle soap he's struggling with and trails after me into my stall. "Dang, you look like something not even the cat would drag in."

"Thanks."

Pug rushes in from one of the other stalls. He's got a pitchfork in his hand. "How much weight have you lost? You look skinnier already."

I drop onto my cot. The rusty springs creak under me, and the bouncing makes me a little queasy. I pull the blanket off and toss it on the pile with all the other sweat-soaked things. A chill grabs me by the shoulders.

"I was talking to one of the other jockeys," Oatmeal says. "Do you know Alabaster Rob?"

"Works for Silverfish Stables, right?"

"That's the guy. He rode Dollars for Donuts in the Stars and Stripes Stakes a few years back. I would've given my whip arm to see that one!"

"I might've given both arms and my left foot," I say.

"Anyhow," Oatmeal says, "Alabaster suggested something called a suppository."

"What's that?" I ask.

"No idea," Pug says.

"He said it's some kind of pill you stick up your butt," Oatmeal says. "From what Alabaster tells me, it'll help you crap off weight like nobody's business."

"Me crapping *is* nobody's business."

"That's for sure," Pug says.

"Where's Fireside?" I ask. "He should be back from his workout by now."

Thinking about that horse alone with anyone other than me brings Jasper to mind. I wonder if he might've gotten to the other exercise boys. Any one of them—Bucky, Oatmeal, or Pug—could sponge Fireside just as easily as me. Two hundred dollars is a heap of money, especially considering all of us are dead broke.

"Mr. Hodge changed things up today," Oatmeal says. "He wanted Fireside to get used to running in broad daylight. He thought it'd help with his jumpiness."

"Did they take him out with the shadow roll?"

"I think so," Pug says. "They wrapped his legs too so the bookies wouldn't recognize his markings—something about Fireside's odds."

"Yeah," I say. "If the bookies see he's running well, they'll lower his odds. It means Mr. Hodge is thinking Fireside's gonna win this race before any of the other horses leave the gate and he wants to surprise everyone. And probably cash in on things himself."

"Jack!" Mr. Hodge's voice shakes the shed walls. He comes into the stall, his hands deep in his pockets. "We need to talk." He flicks his chin to the side, and the other guys take the hint. After Oatmeal and Pug scoot past, Mr. Hodge leans against the doorframe. "How you doing with your weight, son?"

"Okay, I guess. I'm sure I've dropped something. But gosh, Mr. Hodge, ten pounds in two days—it's an awful lot."

"Just stay single-minded on your task," he says. "It's no different than anything else. There ain't no better track in the world to bust your cherry on than Saratoga. This is where some of the best horses in the world have gotten their hats handed to them. Jim Dandy upset Gallant Fox here."

"1930 Travers," I say. "Listening to that race on the radio is what got me thinking a kid like me could become a real jockey someday."

"Well, your day is almost here."

"How's Showboat doing?" I ask him.

Mr. Hodge's head swings back and forth. I don't want to hear the words I know are coming, but they come anyway. "Not so good. Mr. Pelton just got back from the hospital. Showboat'll live, but he won't be riding again, leastways not in any competitive way." Mr. Hodge pulls his cigar from his mouth and rolls it between his fingers, examining it. The moist end glistens with spit. "The doctors think he won't be using his legs no more. I tell you, those starting gates are death traps. Should have left well enough alone."

That's not what I want to hear a day before I'm supposed to load myself into one. No matter how many times I've practiced breaking from them, I don't like the idea of getting into anything Mr. Hodge calls a "death trap."

"What's gonna happen to Showboat? To his wife and his kid?"

"Don't rightly know," Mr. Hodge says. "Maybe, if he improves enough to get up and around, he could do some light breeze work, maybe some more serious training. Lots of guys like him end up becoming agents or working some other light job on the backstretch. Others . . ."

"Others what?"

Mr. Hodge rubs his stubble. "Others don't. Look, son, we try our best to take care of our own around here, but some guys just don't bounce back."

"If you talk to Showboat, tell him there's a collection going around for him down here. Tell him people are putting together what they can."

"Will do," he says. "By the way, your father called." Mr. Hodge changes topics of conversation faster than a bat changes directions in flight. "He said he got stuck down in Albany today. Something about a work opportunity. Apologized over and over again about not being on that train."

Talking about my father makes my stomach flop-flip the way it does when a feisty horse drops out from under me. "My dad's in Albany?"

"Seems so," Mr. Hodge says. "Mind you, I'm getting this secondhand, but I'm told he said all the jobs out in Syracuse dried up and he came out east to see if there was anything down by the docks or at the textile mills."

"The *jobs* in Syracuse?" I say. "We own a farm. What's he need a job for?"

"Suppose I'd know as much about that as I do about those Grand Prix cars you're always going on about. Says he'll try and give you a call in the next few days."

A trickle of sweat makes its way between my shoulder blades, and it's not on account of the heat.

"Look, son." Mr. Hodge squeezes my shoulder like my father did the day he sent me off with Tweed. "You've got a lot on your dinner plate right now, but you've got to get all that other business out of your head. Forget about Showboat. Forget about your father. All that matters these next few days is horse racing. All that matters is making weight." He squares my shoulders to himself and adds, "Be-Do-Achieve."

"Huh?"

"Be-Do-Achieve," he says again, this time more slowly. "It's what every jockey needs to understand."

"What's it mean?"

"It means you got to *be* the person you want to be so that you can *do* the things you need to do so that you can *achieve* the things you want to achieve."

I try to let the words make sense in my head, but the more I think about them the more jumbled and confused they all seem.

"Racing is all about Be-Do-Achieve." Mr. Hodge taps the side of his head. "Let's say for example you wanted to win the Kentucky Derby. How's that sound?"

"How's that sound? That sounds great."

"Right, well, dreaming about winning the Kentucky Derby isn't going to get you one hair closer to winning it. Dreaming ain't going to get you squat. But, if you *become* the sort of person who wins the Kentucky Derby, you'll start *doing* the sorts of things that Kentucky Derby winners do. Before you know it, you'll be winning race after race and getting closer to what you want. And if you do what you have to do, before you know it you'll be holding that gold trophy above your head and it'll be all you can do to keep those flashbulbs from blinding you."

"You make it sound so easy."

Mr. Hodge chuckles. "It ain't easy. What's easy is being a stall mucker the rest of your life. Mucking stalls, all you have to do is what your boss tells you. All you have to do is shovel shit. When you follow your dreams, you have to please yourself. That ain't easy."

"Be-Do-Achieve," I say. "I'll think on it."

"You do that," Mr. Hodge says. "Now, the first race you're running tomorrow, I've got the whole thing mapped out." He pulls his racing form from his pocket and unfolds it. "I studied this rag all night. I figure the two and the four are the speed horses. I want you to sit third out of the gate. They should go a quarter mile in twenty-three and three-fifths. At the half mile, they should be going forty-eight and small change."

"Rusty Gate can do that with three of her hooves tied together," I say.

"I know it, but don't go leaping out of your britches out there, son. Hold her back and run the times I'm telling you. Sit third." Mr. Hodge's eyes sparkle, and his excitement gets me excited. Thinking about being on Rusty Gate in a real race makes everything else I'm worrying about drop away.

"The four horse should peter out somewhere around six furlongs," he says. "That'll put you in second."

I can tell from the way he's looking at me like I'm not even there that Mr. Hodge can see the whole race in his head.

"As you make that final turn, all you'll see is that two horse's rear end, and you know how Rusty Gate don't like eating dust. Give her a tap or two right then and get her to change lead legs. I don't think you'll have a problem after that. You got it?"

I nod. Changing lead legs means urging a horse to switch which of its front legs strikes the ground first. Getting the horse to do that usually takes a shift of my weight to the left or the right. It gives the horse an extra boost of energy because it'll be reaching out with its less fatigued leg. If you can get a horse to switch leads at the right time, it makes all the difference in the world.

"What about Lucky Chance in the fifth?"

"You let me chew on that one for a while." Mr. Hodge lets out a chuckle. "That race is gonna be a mite bit harder. It's a tougher field, and you're riding a weaker horse. I want you thinking about Rusty Gate right now. I want you running through everything I told you over and over until it's branded into your brain. You have to know how that race is going to unfold before you even get up on that horse. You got to see it. You got to feel it. You got to smell it."

"Sure thing, Mr. Hodge." I have no idea what smelling a race has to do with winning it—most races smell like dirt and horse sweat—but there's no upside in telling him that.

"Now, I need to talk to you about Fireside."

My throat closes up. "What about him?"

"We're running him in a stakes race toward the end of the meet. Bolton Stakes, to be exact. It's a monster of a race, mile and a half. Twenty-thousand-dollar purse. Winner takes all. Anyhow, I've discussed it with Mr. Pelton, and we may want you to ride him."

"Me?"

"That's right." He rolls his cigar between his fingers and places it back between his lips. "It all depends on how you do in the interim, mind you. I'm getting you a few mounts on Thursday, a few on Friday. Then there's next week and the week after. But there ain't anyone I trust on the back of that horse more than you. That shadow roll did him good. It was all Bucky could do just to hang on today. Nipped a full second off his best time."

My teeth clench when I hear Bucky rode Fireside on a record run.

Fireside is the pride of Pelton Stables. The fact that Mr. Pelton and Mr. Hodge want me to debut him here at Saratoga means a lot. They could just as easily hire a top-notch free-lancer to ride him. A veteran jockey would be crazy not to take the mount. Even though he's a little green, Fireside is descended from great stock. Not to mention he's faster than a potbellied pig at slop time.

"Now, son, get back to work at making weight." Mr. Hodge pats me on the arm and leaves his hand resting heavy on my shoulder. After my time with Tweed, I still tense up whenever someone touches me. I step away and grab a dry blanket from the pile in the corner. "I know you can do it," he says.

"Be-Do-Achieve," I say.

"And you better *be* a hundred and six pounds by tomorrow."

"Sure thing, Mr. Hodge."

"That's what I like to hear."

The smell of cigars lingers well after he's gone. I pull an old betting slip from my pocket. I scooped it off the ground on closing day at Belmont. It says, "Apple of Her Eye e/w 66-1." E/W means "each way": win, place, and show. That means the horse can come in first, second, or third place and the bettor will still win money. I liked it only on account of the word "apple." It reminded me of the farm back home. I turn over the betting slip and with my stubby bedside pencil scrawl the words "Be-Do-Achieve" across it. I tack it to the wooden stud next to my cot so I can see the words at night as I lie on my side. Then, I zip up the stinky rubber hot suit and head back into the afternoon heat.

IO

WHEN I STRIP OFF THE RUBBER HOT SUIT, THE AIR touching my skin sends shivers through my whole body. I get on over to the hose at the side of the shed row to rinse off. I can count each rib and see my stomach muscles better than ever. It sure is amazing what a day of calisthenics in a hot suit can do to a guy.

The boys, along with just about everyone else, went down to the commissary to beat the stampede. Me, I don't have the time for that. Heck, I can't risk the chance a half cracker might leap from the table into my mouth.

Compared to the excitement of opening day, today was calm on the backstretch. It's only late afternoon—the sun is still high, still hot—and the horses are quiet as cotton in their stalls. Even Spoons is still. He's usually scurrying and scrabbling all over the place, but right now he's just sitting there on the edge of the roof watching me.

"Congratulations." The gravelly voice makes my shoulders hunch up. It's Jasper. His broad shoulders block out the sun.

A tattoo peeks out of a rolled-up sleeve. It's so faded I can't tell if it's an anchor or a dancing girl. "I heard about your promotion to bug boy," he says. "Sounds like all your problems are solved."

"What problems?" I lower the hose. It gushes water at my feet.

"Every exercise boy's got problems," he says. He lifts a riding crop from his side and begins tapping the wide, flat end in his palm. "Otherwise, you wouldn't be doing what you're doing. You get paid less than a cook in a hobo jungle, and for what?"

"Well, look at you," I say right back. "You're out here begging a dog like me to do something we both know I shouldn't. Who's got more problems?"

"*Begging?* You worthless little—" Jasper surges forward and raises the crop to hit me. He reaches out with his free hand, but his shoes sink into the mud that's pooled up around the spigot. "Get over here!"

Fat chance. I leap back.

The hose falls from my hand and begins squirming around like a newly dug up night crawler. Water sprays everywhere. I try to scramble away, but there's nowhere to run. Jasper has me cornered between the barn and a stack of horseshoe crates. His shoes make sucking sounds as he pulls his feet from the mud. "Brand-new pair of wingtips," he hisses, trying to shake the muck off. First one foot, then the other. "Goddamn you."

He takes his good old time turning off the spigot. Then, he shoves me against the barn and holds me there with a huge hand. The dark wood has been baking all day in the sun, and it scorches my shoulders. "Look, kid, I tried the nice way. I fed you and asked all polite like, but it don't look like the nice way works with an idiot like you. Now we do this my way."

My fingers claw at his, but I can't pry them loose.

"You're going to sponge that horse," he says. Each word comes out slow and measured, like his saying it softer will get me to understand better. "You're going to sponge him like I told you, and no one is going to be the wiser. If you snitch to your boss or that old trainer, or if you decide not to do it at all, you're going to disappear. It's that simple." Jasper smiles a thin smile that looks like someone put it there with a brand-new straight razor. "And if you think anyone is going to come looking for you, you're mistaken. You are a bug boy—a worth-less bug boy. No one'll blink twice."

Jasper pulls the sponge from his pocket and presses it into my hand. It fills my fist. "And just so you don't forget, I'm gonna give you a little advance reminder."

He presses me harder against the side of the barn. I swear I can hear my skin sizzle on the hot wood. Then he pulls back his other hand, the one holding the riding crop. His fingers squeeze around it, and he lifts his arm high.

I squeeze my eyes shut.

But the swat never comes.

Jasper's hand leaves my bare chest, and I hear him grunt. My shoulders peel off the barn. When my eyes open, Jasper is lying in the mud. A trickle of blood makes its way from his nose. Niles is standing over him dancing like a bare-knuckle boxer.

"Now, you stay away from Mr. Jack," Niles says to Jasper. "You stay away from this whole darn stable. I know you up to no good. If I see you round here again, you'll have worse to deal with than a busted nose on top of your broken one."

Jasper stands up. He presses the back of his hand to a nostril and checks for blood. His gray trousers are covered in mud, and it's the first time I notice he's not wearing any socks. Bare feet in black wingtips. What kind of guy wears a suit with no socks? Jasper studies the red stain on his hand and grins. His teeth are pink with blood, and he spits into the mud. "Looks like I'll be dealing with a worthless bug boy *and* a ni—"

But Niles steps forward, and his glare stops that awful word from passing Jasper's lips.

"Get out of here, Jack," Niles says to me. "Just go on and get yourself out of here."

I squeeze the sponge in my fist and take a few steps away. "You sure I shouldn't—"

"Get out of here," Niles says. "I'll take care of this."

I don't say another word and run back to the barn, only stopping to stuff Jasper's sponge into a trash bin. The dimness of the stall swallows me, and I begin to feel safe, like a bear in its den. But then I realize this could be the least safe place I could be. Everyone knows this is where I stay, where I sleep. I'm completely exposed here.

Bucky is just getting back too. He sprawls across my bed in his grimy clothes and starts flipping through a comic book that was lying on my pillow. "That Fireside sure is a loaded pistol," he says. "Heck, he's a loaded cannon. He's a rocket ship like in this here Buck Rogers adventure."

"That's for sure," I mutter. My hands are still shaking, but I manage to zip myself into the rubber suit and suck a few drops of water from a rag.

"You okay?" He peers over the comic at me. "Your face is red. Maybe you should take it easy a little."

"No time to take it easy," I say. "Hey, you want to come down and check weight with me? I need a change of scenery." The truth is I'd rather be at the dentist getting all my teeth drilled with rusty tools than sit around the barn right now.

"Hell yeah," Bucky says. "I've never been in the jockeys' room before!"

THE JOCKEYS' LOUNGE IS THE ROOM where the horsemen wait between races. I'm looking forward to seeing if things are even half as crazy as I've heard on race days, but being that the last race is long over, the place is deserted. Rows of lockers line the dark-paneled walls, and sofas and armchairs point every which way. A door in one corner is labeled "Sweatbox." The door next to it is labeled "Dr. Baumstumpf." A card table sits in the middle of the room, and the Oracle sits on the far side.

Although the lounge is appointed nicer than any horse stall, it's not a place I'd want to spend a lot of time in. It smells like years of old sweat and mildew. Being here makes me feel like I'm locked inside a stuffy steamer trunk.

"This place is aces," Bucky says. He runs his hand along the lockers. "Someday, one of these is going to have my name on it, right on a brass plate in big letters. Bucky Sorensen it'll say."

"This room makes me feel like I'm choking."

"Are you kidding me? This room means you've hit ten grand slams!"

I strip to my drawers and step up to the Oracle. Its long, notched sliders remind me of a toothy grin—like the scale is sharing a joke with someone standing behind me. A wave of queasiness washes over me, and I hold Bucky's shoulder to steady myself. I step on the cold metal plate. It shifts side to side, but I get my balance and let go of him. Bucky nudges the weights until the arm sinks down to the hatch mark.

"A hundred and twelve pounds," I say. "I've lost four. That means I still have another six to go."

"That's great," Bucky says.

"No it's not!" I snap at Bucky, a touch nastier than I intended. "Look at me! I don't have anything left to lose."

"We could cut off your arm."

I smile at that and pull the rubber suit back on. The stench of the old, sweaty rubber makes my head cloud up. Dizziness creeps in from the sides, but a few deep breaths help to fight it off. I zip up, suck a few drops of water from a wet rag, and head back out to the track for more laps.

II

I SQUEEZE THE REINS TIGHTLY WITH BOTH HANDS AND shift from side to side in the stirrups to make sure my toes are perched perfectly on the pegs. My rear nestles into the strip of leather and sheepskin they call a racing saddle, and my knees press up into my chest. My mount shifts nervously, blowing out her nostrils as she stomps in the starting gate. Someone has braided two ribbons, one purple and one white, in her hair. Was it Niles? Was it Bucky?

I look to each side and see eight other jockeys—seven to the right, one to the left—lined up just like I am. That's strange. They are all wearing purple silks just like mine; their horses' manes are all braided with the same purple and white ribbons. Nine jockeys all wearing Pelton's colors? How can that be? I try to get a look at their faces, but something blocks each one—a post, a shoulder, a turn of the head.

"Hey!" I call to the starting official. "Pelton can't be running every horse in this race. It's against the rules."

"He locked it up," the starter says. "Pelton runs everything."

I lean forward to get a look at one of the other jockeys. Who could Mr. Pelton have hired? A bunch of freelancers? Did he bring on a bunch of new contract riders? I wonder if these are people I know. And that's when the jockey to my right turns his head. It's a face I recognize, all right. I recognize it because it's my own. It's me. One by one, the seven jockeys to my right turn their heads, and every last one of them is me. All of them are me.

I squeeze my reins tight and suck in a breath.

I turn to the left to check the jockey over there. He's staring right at me. His face fills my entire field of vision like he's poised inches from my eyes. It's a face I know better than my own. It's a face I won't ever forget.

It's Showboat.

His helmet, split into fragments, rests on his head. Blood trickles down his cheeks in rivulets. Smeared. Flowing. It stains his silks so they appear not purple and white but brown and ruby.

"Hey there, Jack," Showboat says. His yellow teeth are slick with blood. "Nothing like cashing in on another guy's hard luck, huh?"

I want to leap from the saddle, to dash from the starting gate screaming, but I know I can't. I have a race to run. Too many people are depending on me.

Showboat's face dissolves. It gets dark. It gets even darker.

Am I asleep?

I hear voices.

Are the voices arguing?

No.

No, they're just talking.

But there's concern in those voices.

Something smells terrible.

Where am I?

I try to open my eyes. The light is so bright I have to squint. Then, I squeeze my eyes shut altogether.

The voices stop.

I've seen photographs of Death Valley out in California. The ground there is so dry that the soil can't soak up any rainwater. It rolls right across and gets baked off again. That's how my mouth feels. That's how my whole body feels.

Someone pushes a wet cloth between my lips. Water. Cold water. I suck on it and let the fluid slide around my mouth. I suck harder. I try to swallow, but my throat won't listen. No place to go, the water dribbles down my cheek.

"Just relax, my boy."

I don't recognize the voice. It's deep and has some kind of thick accent. Maybe German. I try to open my eyes, but the light is still too bright.

"Sorry about that," the voice says.

The light clicks off, and the red glow in my eyelids goes dark. I open my eyes as much as I can. Everything is blurry, but I see a wide-chested man standing over me. The tag on his lab coat says "Dr. Baumstumpf." I'm on an examination table. Bucky, Oatmeal, and Pug are sitting on the edge of a bench against the opposite wall. I suck on the cloth some more. The heat in my throat cools off just a little.

It smells like manure, but really strong, like I'm swimming in it. I want to ask why it stinks so bad, but I can't get the words out.

Dr. Baumstumpf's heavy hand rests on my shoulder. It's more the hand of a mechanic or a farmer than a doctor. "Relax," he says as he eases me back. "Give your body a chance." I do.

SOMEONE IS STROKING MY FOREARM.
It feels nice.
I let them keep doing it.

THE FACT THAT I'M AWAKE creeps in around the edges.
What time is it? How long do I have before weigh-in?
Someone is still stroking my forearm.
It still feels nice.
I hoist my eyelids to see who's there.
It's Bucky. He's staring down at me, stroking my arm over and over again.
I yank my hand away. "My name's Jack, not Janet," I manage to say. My voice sounds like it's coming from a dying frog. I try to sit up on the exam table, but everything spins. I drop back to my elbows. Oatmeal and Pug are gone. So is Dr. Baumstumpf.
Bucky curls his hands into balls. "Sorry, I just thought—"
"You just thought what?"
"I don't know. I just thought that's what I'd like if I was the one passed out on a doctor's exam table. My mom used to do it for me if I had a real bad fever. That was before . . ."
"Bucky—" But I let it go. I don't want to start prying open his box of memories. I sure wouldn't want him prying open mine. "Where are the other guys?" I say. "Where's the doctor?"
"Oatmeal and Pug, they're back at the barn. They had to

finish up in the stalls. Without you, everything's taking twice as long. Dr. Baumstumpf said he was going down to the Union Hotel for a cocktail. Said he'll be back later to look in on you."

The Union Hotel? People go to the Union after dinner.

"What time is it? How long have I been here?"

"I dunno. It's somewhere after six. You've been out for two or three hours—maybe more. How much do you remember?"

I think back. I remember Jasper and his offer. I remember Elizabeth telling me about her bookmaking business. I remember her giving me her telephone number at the Adelphi. My hand moves to my pocket to find the slip of paper she gave me, but I can't find my pocket. I'm wearing one of those blue patient gowns. I remember going to the train station to meet my father. He didn't show. Mr. Hodge spoke to me about the race, and I remember standing up there on the Oracle. I still have six pounds to lose.

"Six more pounds." The words escape my lips before I have a chance to think on anything else.

"Can't be that much," Bucky says. "After you left the jockeys' lounge with me, you ran that track until you dropped. We lost count of how many times you went around, but jeez, you kept going like some kind of machine. I can't believe anyone could hold that much sweat!"

"What's that smell?" I finally ask. "Why's it stink like manure in the doctor's office?"

"That's something you'll probably laugh about with us someday."

"What?"

"Of all the places you could've passed out, Jack."

I know what Bucky is going to say before he says it, and I know this is one I'm never going to live down.

"You passed out facedown in one of the carts. All we could see were your feet sticking out the back." He points to a pile of clothes in the corner that's so covered in filth it looks like a huge heap of dung. "We stripped you, and the nurse washed you a little, but we gotta get you in a shower."

Even for me, the thought of diving headfirst into horse manure is sickening. I would throw up if there were anything left in my stomach. I try to stand, but the dizziness grabs hold of me again.

"Oh, here." Bucky hands me a glass of water from a metal cart. "The doctor said you should drink in tiny sips and suck on some orange rinds."

"Orange rinds?"

"Something to do with minerals." Bucky shrugs. "I have no idea. Any time a doctor starts talking to me, my brain shuts down and goes on a cruise. I don't understand any of that medical hoo-ha. All I can tell you is he ate the oranges and left the peels for you."

"Orange peels. Great."

I snatch the glass from Bucky. The water sloshes out and runs down my hand. I struggle to make my throat do what it doesn't want to do and drink every drop in three gulps. The liquid makes my stomach stretch tight. Coldness presses at the base of my throat. At least everything stays inside. Bucky hands me an orange rind, and I place it on my tongue. It tastes strange, like a fistful of nails.

"Oatmeal and Pug, they took your rubber suit and the dirty blankets back to the barn. They said they'd start the laundry." Bucky stands up. "The question is, How're we going to get *you* back to the barn? You can't put those clothes back on."

I tug at my patient gown. "I suppose I'll have to wear this."

"I don't even have a jacket for you, so it looks like your lily-white ass will be swinging in the breeze."

"It doesn't seem like I have much of a choice," I say. "The faster I can get back into that hot suit, the faster I'll drop the weight."

"We should get going then," he says. "We're gonna be up late tonight."

"We?" The thought of more exercise, of having to lose even more weight, makes me want to collapse right there—to roll over and pass out. I put another orange rind in my mouth and begin chewing. Did I swallow the last one?

"We," Bucky says. He smiles a toothy smile. "You don't think I'd leave you on your own to make weight for your first day of racing, do you? If you're staying up all night, I'm staying up all night. I'll match you squat thrust for squat thrust."

"That sounds lewd," I say.

Bucky's face goes red. "They're exercises, stupid!"

"I know, but it still sounds lewd."

Bucky grins at that. He's the closest thing to family I have around here. With track workers being a rung or two above carnival folks and carnies being a rung above pickpockets and petty thieves, finding a true friend in this line of work is a rare thing. Everybody is so cutthroat it gets in the way of growing close to anyone. The track is definitely a "me first" kind of place.

With Bucky, Oatmeal, and Pug, things are different. We all swore in blood that if any of us hit it big, we'd do everything we could to bring the other three up along with us. Even though all us kids got is our word, sometimes I wonder whether Oatmeal's or Pug's glue would actually stick. With Bucky, there's no doubt. That kid is loyal through and through.

I sit on the edge of the exam table. The leather feels cool on the backs of my thighs. My head spins a little, but I manage to stay up. "I have to tell you something, Buck, but you have to promise not to say anything. You can't say nothing to no one."

Bucky's head cocks to the side. He moves closer and locks his eyes on mine. "Sure thing, Jack."

"I'm not kidding here. You have to swear on your life."

Bucky crosses his heart. "On my life," he says.

"Do you remember a hinky-looking goon at the barn yesterday? He came around after I exercised Fireside."

"Everyone around here is hinky-looking," he says. "Now that I think about it, everyone around here's a goon too. If they're not hinky-looking or they're not a goon, I start getting nervous."

"Come on," I say. "You remember him. He was wearing a gray suit, and his face was bashed in like it met the business end of a sledgehammer."

"Nope."

I pop another orange rind in my mouth. "Don't you remember how I disappeared for a while after coming in from breezing Fireside?"

Bucky shakes his head.

"You don't remember mucking Fireside's stall for me? Me coming back with a white handkerchief and the other guys ribbing me about it?"

"Oh yeah," Bucky says. "That was sort of funny."

"Yeah, that Oatmeal's a real stitch," I say. "Anyway, the guy I went off to talk with, his name's Jasper. He works for one of the other owners."

"Really? Which one?" Since all the big horse owners follow the racing from track to track, meet to meet, we get to know the different stables pretty well.

"I'm not sure," I say. I take Dr. Baumstumpf's rubber hammer from the metal cart and tap at my bare knee. My foot jerks forward and then swings freely. "He wouldn't tell me. Anyhow, this Jasper guy is tougher than a boiled owl. He offered me some serious money to sponge Fireside."

"Sponge him? You mean like wash him down? Like the nurse did to you? That's weird."

I tap his forehead with the hammer. "Not wash him down. Sponging a horse means shoving a sponge up his nose so he can't breathe so good. It slows the horse up." Even though I only learned about sponging the day before, I say it like I've known my whole life.

"How much money did he offer?"

I know it's not such a great idea to share this with Bucky, but I've already told him enough to get me tossed out for good. I don't see why the amount matters. "Two hundred bucks," I say.

Bucky's eyes almost pop out of his head. "Holy moly!"

"Holy moly's right."

"What did you do?" he asks.

"I told him to shove off. I don't want to get mixed up with a guy who ain't hitting on all eight cylinders."

"Probably smart," Bucky says. He wraps my dirty clothes in a clean towel and tucks the bundle under his arm like he's carrying a loaf of bread rather than a heap of crap. "But that sure is a lot of money."

"I know it."

"It's enough money to . . ." His hand grasps in front of him as though he might be able to snatch the answer out of the air with his fingers. "It's enough money to I don't know what!"

I lower my feet to the tile. The floor is cold and a little sticky. Slowly, I shift my weight to my legs. At first, they feel wobblier than a newborn foal's, but once I stand up and get moving, they begin to get steadier.

Bucky grabs my elbow and helps me balance. "What would you do if you came into two hundred dollars like that?" He leads me back into the jockeys' lounge.

"I'm not sure," I say. "I'd probably go home for a while. Two hundred bucks is around a year's salary."

"You can't go home!"

"I'm not going anywhere," I say right back. I have to make this clear for Bucky. There can be no misunderstanding. "Like I said, I'm not taking a dime of that money. I'm not sponging Fireside." Just saying it makes me feel better, like the words alone can make my will stronger.

Bucky keeps his hand clenched on my arm. With me in a patient gown and him leading me by the elbow, I can't help but think of a father walking a bride down the aisle. That thought, along with Bucky touching me, makes me feel squirmier than I already am.

"But if you did take the money, you couldn't leave," he says. "What would happen to us? You're the one what keeps us all in line."

"What would *you* do with that kind of money?" I ask. I figure getting him thinking about himself might get him to stop thinking about me so much.

Bucky chews on my question for a minute. "Wow," he says. "Two hundred bucks. I think I'd get myself a whole new outfit. You know, nice trousers, nice shirt, and new suspenders. I'd get a new hat too. Everything. I'd buy the shiniest wingtips you've ever seen. Then, I'd rent a car and have the driver take all us guys—me, you, Oatmeal, and even Pug—for a night on the town." Bucky's eyes open wide like he can see it all. "We'd go to the casino and shoot dice, and we'd have the thickest steaks you've ever seen!"

At the mention of steak, my stomach twists in knots. "You mind not talking about food?" I say.

"Oh, yeah—sorry. But wow, two hundred smackeroos!"

"Remember, you can't say nothing. You can't say nothing to nobody."

"Jack, I might be stupid, but I ain't that stupid."

I shuffle over to the Oracle. Just like last time, the shiny metal sliders grin past me. The weights are still sitting where we left them—one hundred and twelve pounds. This time I'm just plain curious how much weight I burned off while I was in a complete daze. When I stand on the plate, the slider doesn't jump. That's a good sign. At least I've lost something. Bucky taps the smaller of the two weights little by little until the pointer lifts and settles on the hatch mark.

I step off the plate, grab my patient gown, and wrap it around myself.

"A hundred and ten," Bucky says. "That's great. You've lost like six pounds!"

"Four more to lose in fourteen hours and you say that's great?" I hate snapping at Bucky, but the words just burst out.

He shrugs. "You can do it, Jack. I know you can."

I'm not a big guy to start with, but I'm the lightest I've been since I was eleven years old. I catch a look in a mirror hanging on the wall. At first I don't recognize myself. My cheeks are sunken like those of an old, toothless codger. My ribs look like glockenspiels on either side of my chest. I can't imagine dropping another four pounds. Where would it come from? I have to find time to sleep too. If I'm going to ride in two races tomorrow, I need some strength. I need to be alert. Riding a race ain't no stroll down the backstretch.

The next thing I know, my gut tightens and the muscles in my stomach bend me in two. The water I just guzzled down spews out of my mouth, burns the inside of my nose. It splatters on the floor of the jockeys' lounge and onto my bare feet and ankles. The clear liquid runs under the front edge of the Oracle.

Bucky claps me on the back as I sink to my knees over my vomit. Small bits of orange rind float in the sour-smelling puddle. "Good man," he says. "Probably only three pounds now."

12

MY HEAD IS FILLED WITH CRUSHED GLASS. WHEN I squint against the pain, shards stab at the backs of my eyes.

"Hey," one of the jockeys in line with me says. "Give the new kid the up-and-down."

"I doubt he'll make it out of the gate, let alone round the track," another says.

"Ten bucks to your one says he won't even make it up into the saddle," yet another chimes in.

The paddock is a grassy area off to the side of the picnic grounds. It's enclosed by a white wooden fence, which opens to a chute that leads to the track. Even with all the horses, trainers, owners, and jockeys milling around back here, there's still plenty of room to breathe—that is, if I had the strength to suck in air.

One by one, jockeys weigh in and horses are saddled up in front of everyone. Whoever built the track, along with this paddock, must've figured that'd be a good idea—maybe to keep us guys honest. More likely, it's to make everyone believe there's no funny business going on. Half these guys standing around are crookeder than a dozen shepherd's sticks. Things like a paddock make them think up other, even sneakier ways of getting around the rules. And I've seen some doozies.

Thinking about crooked guys brings Jasper to mind. I wonder if he's out there watching me. I wonder what he might be thinking, what he might do next. Then I tell myself to let it go. I don't have the strength to worry. I'm having trouble enough just standing up with all my gear in my hands.

Hundreds of spectators pack around the paddock to watch—to size up the horses and to see the celebrity jockeys. With all the cheering and calling out, it's like a crowded market, but the other jockeys stand around like it's business as usual: signing autographs, shaking hands, and chatting up the young ladies. Like always, the marshals have wheeled the Oracle out into the open, and we're standing in line waiting to weigh in.

I have no idea how I got here, how I'm wearing the purple and white silks of Pelton Stables. I vaguely remember Bucky struggling to push a boot onto my foot, but everything else in my head is fuzzy. Somehow, I always saw this moment differently. If today is my dream coming true, I'd hate to see my nightmare.

My saddle rests across my arms along with my whip and helmet. Although my gear weighs only a few pounds, it feels like a ton. My fingers and toes are numb, and it's all I can do to stay on my feet. I must look like some kind of marionette. When I drift forward, I pull my weight back. When I start leaning back too far, I throw my weight forward. This is no state to be in twenty minutes before a race. In riding, balance is everything, and I've got it in short supply at best.

The sniggering continues as I inch toward the Oracle. I haven't weighed myself since last night, but I only need to weigh one hundred and fifteen pounds for this race. This one is in the bag. My concern is for the next. I'm hoping that even if I'm not at a hundred and six now, riding my first race will help me burn enough for me to hit my mark for the second.

When that scale looms before me, I almost drop to my knees. I should be happy. I should be excited. But the truth is that I'm just hungry. Hungry and weak. Tired. Ready to drop.

"Let's go, boy," one of the marshals says. His black handle-bar mustache is waxed so much it looks as though I could hang my helmet on one side and my riding crop on the other. "Purple and white. Pelton Stables, right?"

I nod weakly.

He marks something down on a clipboard. "New kid, huh?"

I nod again.

"Well, get up on the scale then, peewee."

The plate I need to stand on seems ten feet above me, but someone shoves me from behind and I stumble onto it. I watch as the marshal taps the weight up the slider:

104

tap, tap

106

tap

110

tap, tap

113

tap
118
"Wait, this can't be right," I manage to say. "I was . . ."

"I'm sorry, son. With your gear, you weigh a hundred and eighteen pounds. Are you shooting to be a jockey or a longshoreman? Hell, you missed weight by a mile. Better luck tomorrow."

"Tomorrow?" I say. My knees buckle, and I almost fall off the scale. "Tomorrow won't work. I have to ride today! Mr. Pelton . . . Mr. Hodge . . ."

Then, I hear the laughing. A broad smile spreads behind that marshal's waxy mustache, and he points to my feet. I look down and see a stack of lead plates on the scale next to me.

The marshal claps me on the back. "Just a little joke we play on you freshly laid eggs," he says. "No harm, no foul."

No harm, no foul? Just a few years off my life.

I smile all polite like, figuring most of these other jockeys went through the same thing when they were new. Nonetheless, they're all laughing like it's the riproaringest thing they've ever set their eyes on.

"Billy, get those weights off the scale," the marshal says. He turns to me. "Now, lighten up, kid. Your horse is gonna feel all that tenseness coming through your legs. You're weighing in at a hundred and seven. Load the boy with eight pounds, eight ounces. Congratulations, you've made it to the big time." He claps me on the back again as an attendant slips a bunch of lead bars into my saddle, some on each side.

I stumble off the Oracle and make my way to Rusty Gate. She's a chestnut with a long mane and a perky tail. Sure she's smaller than the average Thoroughbred, but she can really cover ground when she wants to. Mr. Hodge and Mr. Pelton are waiting for me like cornermen waiting for a prizefighter. Mr. Hodge is grinning like I've never seen him grin before. "You look like you were born to wear those silks," he says as he takes my saddle from me. He claps me on the shoulder. "You look damn good."

Mr. Pelton nods in agreement. "Son," he says. He hands me a glass of seltzer water, and I gulp it down. "I know this isn't the way you wanted to get into a real race. I know you and Showboat had something special, but his death—"

"Showboat's dead?" I cry out. I look to Mr. Hodge. His gaze drops to the ground as he rubs his stubble, and I know it's true.

"He passed on last night," Mr. Hodge says matter-of-factly. "The doctors said his spine was crushed. It was a miracle he lived so long. It was a miracle he got to see his wife before he left."

I think about Showboat's wife. I think about the baby. What are the two of them going to do? How will they eat? How could Showboat dying from an accident in a starting gate be any kind of miracle?

Mr. Hodge tucks me under his arm and leads me away from everyone else. "Get all that bad news out of your head," he says to me. "Mr. Pelton didn't mean no harm by what he said, but it was downright stupid of him to bring it up. You've trained with these gates for months now. You've done it countless times and you're damn good at it. You're one of the best goddamn gate jockeys I've ever seen. Focus on the positives here, Jack." He runs through the game plan we discussed yesterday and has me recite it back to him.

"Start third out of the gate," I say. "Take out the number four horse after six furlongs, switch lead legs at the final turn, and let the reins loose for the win."

"You got it. This is your race, Jack, so go ahead and take what's yours. It's time for the rest of the world to know what we already know—that Jack Walsh is a top-notch jockey, someone to be reckoned with."

"Be-Do-Achieve," I say.

Mr. Hodge grins, and a hunk of ash falls from the end of the cigar. "That's right," he says. "Be-Do-Achieve."

I nod like I understand, but actually I'm just numb. Mr. Hodge makes it sound so much easier than I know it's going to be, but in the state I'm in, I just want this race to be over with. I can't believe Showboat's dead. He's dead, and just two days after his injury I'm going to be loaded into the very same machine that killed him. Wearing the very same colors.

I'm looking for a spot to sit a minute when a stunning vision in flowers meets my eyes. Elizabeth is standing on the other side of the fence in a pink dress. Her hat has a huge brim, and it's loaded up with white hydrangeas like the ones my mother tends next to the porch. I can't help but notice how the small tree behind her with its low-hanging branches frames her like a photograph. She waves her program at me.

I wave back and excuse myself from Mr. Hodge for a moment.

"Don't let some skirt distract you from the prize, Jack."

"I'll just be a second," I say. "It's Jim Reed's daughter."

"I don't care if it's Cleopatra, the Queen of England, and Miss Helen Hayes all rolled into one," he says. "Don't be more than a minute. We have matters to discuss. In the meantime, I'll get you saddled up."

The closer I get to Elizabeth, the wider her smile gets. "God, you're skinnier than a rake handle," she says.

"Is that supposed to be some kind of compliment?"

"If it's a compliment you're fishing for, how about your purple jacket makes you look less close to death than you probably are."

"That's the best you can do?"

"It's the best you're going to get from me . . ." Her smile turns mischievous. "That is, unless you win."

"Showboat's dead," I say.

Her smile melts away. "It's awful, isn't it?"

"You knew?"

"I found out last night. I was with my father at the Union, and word spread through the club like gossip in a girls' school. I had no way of reaching you. Last I checked, the barns weren't wired for telephones. Anyhow, I wanted you to be fresh for your first race. You can win if you fix your mind on winning."

"I don't know."

She grabs my jacket and tugs me toward her. My chest hits the top rail of the fence, and I can feel everyone staring. "Look, Jack, you have that mark—that little star—next to your name in the program, and that means you're an apprentice rider—a full-fledged bug boy. Starting today, you're riding with professional jockeys. That means you have to start acting like a professional jockey, not some sort of whimpering whelp. Do you understand?"

"I guess."

"You guess?" she says. "Do you think those other jockeys say 'I guess'? Do you think Sonny Workman says 'I guess'? I can tell you one hundred percent for sure that he doesn't, and he's one of the best jockeys around." Then her voice drops low and she says, "Anyhow, I have you at five to one, which is damn good for a first-timer. Best I've ever handicapped."

Maybe it's how the sun is streaming through her hair, maybe it's how she's leaning toward me over the fence, but something about Elizabeth right now reminds me of my mother. The queer thing about it all is that I feel like kissing her too. I feel like kissing her right on the mouth in front of everybody. I look up at her and I realize every word she's saying is right. Every word. Thinking I can't do this is only going to guarantee that I fail. I have to start acting like a jockey. I have to start thinking about winning this race.

"Be-Do-Achieve," I say to Elizabeth.

She looks at me like I'm talking Chinese. "What?"

I answer her with a wink and head back to Mr. Hodge. Strapping on my helmet, I run my hand across its delicate silk covering. The fabric slides under my fingers, cool and smooth. I can feel the thin layer of cardboard underneath. I look down at my silk jacket. Alternating stripes of purple and white, the colors of Pelton Stables. Showboat used to joke about how they reminded him of bars in a prison cell, but to me they mean freedom. I've dreamed of wearing these colors for endless months, any color silks for as long as I can remember, and now the moment is here. I snap my crop against my thigh. The sting feels good.

I place my boot into Mr. Hodge's hand. On the count of three, he boosts me into the saddle on Rusty Gate's back. He's saying something about putting some oil in the hinges of that Rusty Gate and getting her to stop squeaking, but I don't pay no mind. All I can hear are the words in my head:

It's time to be.

It's time to do.

It's time to achieve.

13

DON'T GO SMACKING HER HAUNCHES," I SHOUT AT the starting official. "Let me guide her in." Ever since I got up on Rusty Gate, I've been feeling better—like my body is starting to do what my head is asking of it. Maybe it's all the excitement. Maybe it's the seltzer Mr. Pelton gave me. Either way, a fair amount of the dizziness is gone and some of the strength has come back to my arms and legs.

Rusty Gate seems a little jumpy, but I nose her toward the chute and urge her forward. Thick steel bars crisscross just above where my head's going to be, and I think about Showboat. That's when I get a little jumpy myself. The official at the weigh-in was right; my horse'll sense it if I'm even the least bit nervous. I back her off and turn her around a few times to give us both a minute to breathe.

"Be-Do-Achieve," I tell myself. "Be-Do-Achieve."

I twitch my legs and make a few clicking sounds. Rusty Gate's head perks up like she just now realizes what she's supposed to do. She snorts and moves forward into the chute.

Now, the hard part's going to be keeping her still until all the other horses are in. Being that I'm in the fifth position, there are four more horses that need loading. I pat Rusty Gate's neck as she stomps from side to side. All that stomping and shifting—all that uneasiness—brings Showboat to mind again.

My mind scrambles to think about anything but him, so I think on my family back home. I try to think on each one how I remember them and then try to figure on what they might look like now.

A clang rings out as one of the other horses bumps into the side of the chute. A few of the other jockeys' heads jerk up just like mine, and that calms me down some. These guys are as jumpy as I am. I'm no different than the rest of them. I'm a jockey on a horse and we're all about to run a race at Saratoga.

The crowd seems hushed, but before post time that isn't so out of the ordinary. Most folks aren't paying much attention to what we jockeys are doing, and they sure as sugar aren't cheering. They're busy placing last-second bets or refilling their drinks or chatting with the folks around them. When that bell goes off, though, rest assured, all six thousand pairs of eyes at this here track are going to be on us. And six thousand voices will be screaming, rooting for their favorites.

"Good luck," the jockey to my right says.

"Thanks," I say. I glance at him for a second. I don't recognize him, but he's grinning at me. He's got a friendly smile and friendly blue eyes. As for his age, it's not easy to guess a horseman's age. We're all lighter than a handful of hay and have spent so much time purging that our teeth are gone by age thirty. If I had to guess, I'd figure him for forty or so. That's pretty old for a jockey. He is wearing green and blue silks—the colors of P. J. Teal Stables.

"Linus McCready," he says. "I'd shake your hand, but now's not the best time."

"Mine are shaking too much already," I say.

Then the jockey to my left chimes in. "You better hang on to that scrawny little filly of yours," he says. He's atop the number four horse, the one that Mr. Hodge figures on starting fast but tiring after six furlongs. "New pickles like you always go sour."

I hold out my pinkie and let it curl toward the ground. "If I'm a pickle, then you're a tiny little gherkin," I say. A few of the other riders laugh. "Your horse is going to start sucking wind somewhere toward the end of the backstretch."

The jockey hunches toward me. "All I can tell you is if you want to stay in one piece, you'd better be sure to stay away from me."

"Thanks for the advice," I say. "Will ten lengths ahead be enough?"

"You just wait and see how far your sass gets you around here," he says. But his bold words don't match how weakly he says them. He's got doubts.

The starters already have the eight horse loaded in and are working on the number ten. Being that the nine got scratched, the ten is the last one to load. Once everyone is ready, it's only a matter of seconds before the bell. I lean forward and grab a fistful of Rusty Gate's mane.

The ten horse gives a little trouble, but they get him loaded in no time.

For a brief moment, everything falls silent. The crowd, the

jockeys, even the horses. Rusty Gate twitches under me. My heart is pounding like it's trying to burst out of my chest.

Then, it all happens at once: the bell sounds, the gates slam open, and Rusty Gate fires out of the chute like she's blasting from a cannon. The crowd erupts. The noise is nothing like what I've heard sitting in the stands. When all the voices are aimed toward you, the roar is plain deafening.

Going from zero to forty in two and a half seconds on the back of a Thoroughbred is an indescribable feeling. Even hunched forward like I am, it's all I can do not to topple back and fall to the dirt. When I manage to regain whatever balance I can, I perch on my toes in the irons and crouch even farther over Rusty Gate's mane. Her body lurches forward and back, and her sleek neck lifts toward me with each stride. My knees pound up into my chest as she gallops along with the other horses. We drift toward the rail, vying for position. I'm not used to running in such a tight pack, but Rusty knows what to do.

After a little nudging, I'm sitting third just like Mr. Hodge told me—just behind the number two and number four horses. The pack thins out a little, and we all move tight to the rail. I give Rusty Gate a little slack to put her on a forty-eight-second pace for the half mile. She likes running on the rail, and she picks up the pace smoothly, settling into a nice gallop.

That gherkin on the number four is gaining a pretty good lead. His helmet is bobbing at least four lengths ahead of me. I'm tempted to loosen the reins even more to close the gap, but I know if I ignore Mr. Hodge's game plan I'll probably never be able to ride another horse on account of the foot-

shaped dent he'd plant in my ass. If I follow Mr. Hodge's in-
structions exactly, he can't fault me nearly as bad—even if I
lose.

I pin Rusty Gate's nose on the two horse's tail and let her
run.

As we come out of the turn, I know I'm within a few fifths
of my target time. I allow myself to smile a little. A good jockey
can run a horse eight furlongs—one mile—with less than a
fifth of a second error. Most people find that amazing. To me,
it's simple. I've been doing it for years. What amazes me is
how Mr. Hodge can look at all the tiny columns filled with
numbers on a racing form—how the horse has performed in
past races, in different conditions, at different lengths, with
different gear and different jockeys—and figure out ahead of
time how fast all those other horses are going to run.

The backstretch looks a million miles long, but Rusty Gate
is pulling that earth beneath her like the devil himself is on
her tail. I peek to my right and see another horse inching up.
It's the number six—Linus McCready's horse. With the number two in front of me, I'm risking getting boxed in, so I urge
Rusty Gate a few arms' lengths away from the rail. Linus pulls
up a touch more and moves to the inside, which worries me
because Rusty likes to hug that rail. Not to mention that, if I
stay wide, the far turn is going to wipe my horse out.

A lot can happen in two furlongs, so I try not to get too
concerned.

Just like Mr. Hodge said, the lead horse—the number
four—starts to tire near the sixth post. He begins to drop
back, and I make room by pulling even farther away from the
rail.

"Ta-ta!" I call to the number four jockey as he drops back.

"I'll give you a goddamn ta-ta!" he says. I hear a sharp crack as a searing pain bites into my left thigh. The jockey swings his whip again and connects with Rusty Gate's flank. Startled, Rusty whinnies, puffs hard, and lurches forward. She pours it on until she's neck and neck with the number two.

A cheer surges through the crowd as the announcer barks something—probably about me making a move.

That jockey hitting my horse is a foul—it's downright cheating—but not many fouls are called in racing, especially on the backstretch, where there ain't no officials keeping an eye on us. I tug the reins back in order to slow her up, but if I pull too hard I'll risk losing momentum and the race will be over. That sonofabitch on the number four whips her again. Rusty snorts again and lurches forward.

The crowd cheers like someone is tossing out free money in the grandstands, but anybody who knows horse racing would know I'm in a bad position. With the turn coming up, being this far away from the rail means a few more lengths for my horse to run. Not to mention that Rusty Gate is burning all her energy too soon, galloping faster than I want her to.

I glance back and see that the number four has slowed down enough for me to take in some of the reins without being within whipping distance. Rusty Gate falls behind the number two again, right alongside Linus McCready. Mr. Hodge didn't mention the number six at all, and I have no idea what to expect from McCready. The best I can do is follow the game plan.

"Not bad for your first time out," Linus calls to me.

"Thanks!"

"Don't thank me yet," he says. "The turn's coming up and you're in a tricky position. Live and learn, son!"

As we enter the final turn, I nudge Rusty Gate toward the rail, but Linus pushes us back out. I know staying this wide might spell trouble, but something tells me that dropping back behind the six is the wrong move. I give Rusty a couple of light taps with my whip to squeeze out a few extra ounces of energy and keep her as tight to the inside as I can without risking a foul.

We thunder through the turn, and I sense someone coming up on my right side. I move a little wider to edge them out and lean to the right to let Rusty Gate know to switch lead legs. She does as I ask. She stutters just a little, and I can feel her surge forward. We inch up on the number two's right side and I take Rusty even wider to edge out the horse coming up from behind. The crowd is near to rioting as I move toward the front of the pack, but another horse fills the gap I've made on my left. I came too wide, and Linus took advantage of it.

Just like Mr. Hodge said, the two horse starts to lose steam. It begins to drop back, and Rusty Gate noses out in front. She don't like trailing, that's for sure. The thought that I'm in the lead in the final stretch of a race at Saratoga runs through my mind, but I push it out and focus on the task at hand. "Be-Do-Achieve," I tell myself again. The six is coming on strong, and I give Rusty Gate everything. She's got all the reins, and I'm whipping her with every bit of strength I have left.

Be-Do-Achieve.

Be-Do-Achieve.

Be-Do-Achieve.

I say it over and over again in cadence with Rusty Gate's

hoofbeats. I say it over and over again like a steam engine chugging its way north through the Adirondack Mountains.

I can hear the announcer's nasal voice calling the race, but his words are drowned out by the fans screaming and the hooves pounding dirt. The final post is approaching, and it can't get here fast enough. By the time we cross the finish line, Linus and I are neck and neck, each horse taking the lead with each bob of the head. As soon as we're past, I stand up in my irons and let Rusty Gate slow down at her own pace. Linus keeps abreast of me, and we both glide to a trot. Rusty is blasting like a bellows, and I give her a few pats with my open palm to let her know she's done good.

By the time we loop back, the flag's been raised up the pole to signify the race is going to decision, that it was too close to call and the judges have to discuss the matter. The truth is I already know the result. Both Linus and I know. The moment we crossed that line, the number six horse was stretching forward just a touch more than mine. Linus crossed that line before I did.

Of course, I know better than to say anything. What really happened and what those judges saw are sometimes two entirely different things.

When the decision comes in and the flags go up the pole, I know the judges got the win-place-show positions right: 6, 5, 2. I came in second. I sag in my saddle and head off the track, ready to face Mr. Hodge, ready to face Mr. Pelton.

14

"FIVE BUCKS?" I SAY TO MR. HODGE AS WE MAKE our way across the paddock to the jockeys' lounge. "Five measly bucks? I thought I'm supposed to get ten percent of what my horse takes in. That's got to be twenty or thirty bucks at least."

"Sure, that's what the rules say," Mr. Hodge says, "but this is professional horse racing, son. Ain't much that goes by the rules round here. Can't say I agree with it, but you're a contract worker. None of the contract guys get ten percent."

I want to tear off my gear and toss it in the dirt. I can barely stand on account of starving myself for two days, my leg is on fire from getting whipped across the thigh, and now that bastard Pelton won't pay me the ten percent I've got coming to me because he's too busy sipping fancy champagne in the clubhouse with all the other fat cats.

Mr. Hodge takes off his hat and dabs at his brow with his hankie. "Mr. Pelton does give a ten-dollar bonus for a win, but that's only for a win," he says. "At least as a bug boy you don't

have to go exercising horses all morning or mucking stalls until sundown anymore."

"I guess so."

"You *guess* so?" Mr. Hodge shoves his cigar into his mouth
and puffs on it until a cloud of smoke swallows his head. "You
haven't given any thought to what that means, have you?"

"That I can sleep late?"

Mr. Hodge smirks. He knows I know what it means. It
means I can freelance. I can breeze other stables' horses. And
that pays—usually to the tune of a buck a horse. It also means
I can chase down trainers all morning and try to get freelance
mounts. That's where the money is for guys like me. That's
where I do get my ten percent.

I know I should be happy—heck, I can breeze a dozen
horses a day while reading the paper and sipping a cup of
tea—but I can't help but wonder what Bucky, Oatmeal, and
Pug are going to think. None of them is going to have the
slightest idea of what to do around the stable without me running the show. And like Bucky said, everything takes twice as
long without me.

"So what's this fiver for?" I hold up the bill Mr. Hodge
handed me. "Payday ain't until Friday."

"That five's not from Pelton. It's from me. I had twenty on
Rusty Gate across the board. You did real good out there, son.
Bring that girlfriend of yours out to dinner."

My goggles practically steam up when Mr. Hodge calls
Elizabeth my girlfriend, but I can't seem to stop myself from
glancing around the paddock for her. She's nowhere to be
seen. I'd have figured she'd be standing right around here
someplace. "She's not my—"

"Oh, pshaw," Mr. Hodge says. "Now get the thought of

money out of your head. We'll talk about it later. You did good out there. Yeah, you pulled a little wide on the homestretch, but you did a bang-up job for a first-timer. Be proud of what you've done."

"I could've won that one," I say.

"Now that's the attitude I want you to have." Mr. Hodge puts his hand on my back and pulls me to his side. "But, son, you placed in your first race at Saratoga. You beat seven other jockeys just now, and not a single one of them is a slouch. You've got a lot to be proud of, Jack. Don't let anyone take that away from you."

He's right. I think about how I sped around that track on top of Rusty Gate, about nudging those other horses out of my way, about taking a lash to the leg without forgetting the plan, about taking advantage of every little opportunity. And next time I'll do better.

"It's time to think about your next race," Mr. Hodge says. "You have nearly an hour layoff, so go get yourself cleaned up. Get changed and get ready to weigh in again. We'll talk strategy after that. Right now, I've got to see about our horse in the third."

Mr. Hodge heads back toward the paddock. They hired a freelancer to ride Eager Beetle in the next race. Mr. Hodge is probably off to talk with him about how to go about winning it. I watch him let himself into the jockey paddock and shake hands with a guy I don't recognize. He's wearing the same color silks as I am. Fans lean over the fence to get autographs from riders and trainers and owners who are not me.

And for the first time in a long while, I'm alone. What was a whirlwind of excitement seems like ancient history. The race is over, and all the energy, all the tingling in my arms and legs and the buzzing in my head, disappears. It's time to move ahead. It's time to think about what comes next.

I can do this.

At least I think I can do this.

No, I can definitely do this.

I trudge toward the building that houses the jockeys' lounge and pull off my goggles and helmet. Both are caked with mud. I drag the goggles across my sleeve, which only makes the mud smear worse. A flash of white catches my eye as someone pushes a program under my nose. Tiny fingers grip the pages, and I see a young girl, a girl no more than six, standing before me. Her hat seems twice as wide as her shoulders, and it casts a shadow around her that could swallow her skinny body ten times over. Her patent leather shoes have lost their shine from all the dust.

"May I have your autograph?" she asks. Her huge green eyes stare up at me. She seems nervous—nervous to talk to *me*. Her program touches my arm, and I realize it's not often I talk with someone smaller than myself.

I kneel down so we're eye to eye, and she lets out a deep breath she was holding in. Over her shoulder I see a man and woman who could only be this girl's parents. She's got her father's eyes and her mother's round face. The couple is dressed nice, but not nearly as nice as Mr. Pelton or any of the folks up in the clubhouse.

"I haven't got a pen," I tell her.

"That's okay. I've brought one of my own." The girl pushes a pen into my hand and says, "My name's Lucy and I think you should write: 'To my biggest fan, Lucy. Best Wishes. Jack Walsh.' " She smiles wide, and I see the tip of her tongue poke through the gap where a front tooth used to be.

I scribble what she told me right next to my name. It's the first time I've had a chance to take a look at today's program. I'm not used to getting any attention, let alone seeing my name spelled out right next to those of all the famous jockeys I've been following for years. It feels strange to see that little star next to my name telling folks that I'm an apprentice jockey—that I'm a bug boy. That star is what gives us bug boys our nickname, on account of it looking something like a bug. I draw long legs on the star and a little mean face on top and scrawl the words "Bug Boy" next to it.

I hand the program back to Lucy and see the smiles plastered across her and her parents' faces. I give the man and woman a wink, and they both smile wider. Lucy pulls the program to her chest. She runs back to her folks and gets lost in the folds of her mother's dress.

It's the first autograph I've ever given. I can't believe someone would want it, but for once I feel like I matter around here. Nevertheless, the feeling leaves as quick as it came. I placed second in a race. That's nothing special. It's only a matter of time before they figure out I'm a fraud. It's only a matter of time before people start saying how my name is a smudge on that program.

"Not bad for a guy who ran way too wide on the turn!" a voice calls to me as I'm just about through the door to the jockeys' lounge.

It's Bucky. I'd love to tell him all about the race, every last fifth of a second of it, but I have a lot to do and not a lot of time to do it in. I open the door and wave him inside. If he wants to talk, he's going to have to do it while I get washed up and changed.

"You're covered in mud," he says.

"So you noticed."

"Actually, you look like a walking pile of crap." Bucky scampers down the hallway ahead of me. A dozen or so idle jockeys are sitting in the lounge. A group is playing cards, a few are reading, and one in the corner is sleeping with his feet on the arm of a sofa. Dr. Baumstumpf's door is open, and I see him talking to a jockey who is sitting bare-chested on the exam table.

Bucky snaps his fingers in front of my nose. "So anyhow, Jack, I was thinking—"

"I hope you didn't hurt yourself," I say.

"Hurt myself?"

"You know, hurt yourself thinking."

"Very funny." He grabs hold of my crop and goggles and moves toward the basin to rinse them off. "Anyhow, I was thinking that maybe I could be your valet, you know, help you get ready for the races and clean up your stuff and make sure you've got the right silks for the right races—all those things you won't have time to take care of yourself."

"I don't know," I tell him. "I don't have any money to pay you. Not to mention, you've got so much to do back on the shed row. It's already going to be twice as hard without me. What'll happen to the other guys?"

"Don't you worry about the guys and me," Bucky says. "Now that you're moving up, it's only a matter of time before Pelton hires another kid. Then, Oatmeal and Pug will have someone to push around, someone to make do the hard stuff."

"I suppose so."

"Anyhow, once you get yourself an agent," Bucky says, "he'll be setting you up on all sorts of mounts. The money will be bangin' down your stall door just for the honor of hopping in your wallet. There's plenty to go around. So how about it? Let me valet for you."

"Like I said, Buck, I'm not sure." And really I'm not. I have no idea if I need a valet. I don't even know if I need an agent. I've always focused on riding. I've focused on riding and on taking care of horses and keeping the stalls clean. I haven't ever thought about the business of being a jockey. Now that I am one, I have no idea what to do or what to expect.

I glance around the room, and it's the first time I notice that each flashy, silk-wearing jockey seems to have a shabby counterpart scurrying around like some kind of Christmas elf—polishing boots, hanging uniforms, piling up gear—you name it. If those guys have valets . . .

"I guess it's okay," I say to Bucky as I sit on the bench in front of the locker that had been assigned to me. It was empty when I got here this morning—when one of the workers showed me where to put my street clothes. I wonder if this might have been Showboat's locker. His name isn't on any of the others.

"Good," Bucky says. He kneels in front of me and starts tugging at one of my mud-caked boots. "Because I already told Mr. Hodge I'm going to do it."

"You shouldn't've gone and done that, Bucky. What if things go south? I don't want you to lose your spot with Pelton on account of me."

"What's not to work out?" Bucky says as my boot comes free. He topples backward and slams into my locker. "Things'll work out for sure. Anyhow, what have I got to lose? I've got no future as a jockey, but being a valet . . . there's something I can do."

One of the jockeys at the card table chuckles. "Looks like you already found yourself a lapdog," he says. It's the jockey who was riding the number four horse, the guy who whipped me across the leg and hit Rusty Gate all those times. The lash across my thigh flares up. I want to smack him across the knuckles with my crop, but all I do is nod back. I don't need to get in any scrapes my first day here. I can wait until tomorrow for that.

I strip off my shirt and pants and notice the welt forming on my thigh. It's long and narrow, widening just a bit at the end where the broad part of the leather caught me. The welt is bright pink, but I can tell it's going to darken by tonight.

The jockey drops his cards on the table and stands up. When he sees my leg, he chuckles again. "Hey, no hard feelings," he says. "Part of being a bug boy is knowing your place. You haven't earned the right to talk back to me, or any of the other jocks here—not until you've paid your dues."

None of the others look up. The welt on my leg stings. It stings bad.

"Maybe I'll think about showing you some respect when you beat me," I mutter.

A few of the jockeys chuckle, heads down.

"What was that, bug?" The jockey strides across the room and faces me. He's smaller than I am, but the fire in his eyes makes him seem like a giant.

"You heard me," I say. I grab the latch to my locker and tug at it, but the jockey slams the door shut with his shoulder.

He glares at me, letting the silence say more than words could. The clean area where his goggles had been makes his blue eyes seem brighter than they really are. "Watch who you're mouthing off to," he says.

"That's the problem," I say. "I don't know who you are." I yank at my locker door again. The force of the pull shoves the jockey back. As the door swings open, a flash of brown drops from the locker to my feet, and I hear a sound like a soggy sack of oats landing heavy on the floor.

The jockey leaps back. "What the hell is that?"

I look down to where he's pointing. It's Spoons. It's Spoons, my spider monkey. His head sits crooked on his shoulders, and his purple and white striped silk jacket is yanked askew. His usually soft, pinpoint eyes are gaping wide. They stare up at the ceiling. Dead eyes.

A name almost passes my lips, but I swallow it back down. *Jasper.*

15

THE TROUBLE WITH TAKING A NAP IN A HORSE STALL instead of one of the boardinghouses or the YMCA is that I can never shut out all the daylight or all the noise. I'm too upset, too hungry, too excited, and too worried to sleep anyway. Thoughts stampede through my head so quickly, it's impossible to keep my eyes closed more than a few seconds. I can hear Fireside through the thin wooden slats stomping and shifting around in his stall. He seems just as restless as I am.

When I got back from the track, I could tell Jasper had been here. My stall door was wide open, my cot was flipped, and everything in my crates was tossed. I could smell the stink of his aftershave on everything too. *Did Jasper climb up on my cot to grab Spoons? Did he snap his neck right here in front of Fireside? How much did the little guy suffer?* I push those thoughts from my head and try to set my mind on how the rest of the day went.

It's a miracle, but somehow I won my second race. I crossed the wire out in front by four and a half lengths. With

Showboat, Jasper, and poor Spoons on my mind, not to mention the fact that I could barely see straight on account of not eating for days, I almost decided to quit Thoroughbred racing altogether. I stood there in the shower in the jockeys' lounge for as long as I could and tried to sort through everything. Finally, I decided that running away would be the worst thing I could do. It would be the same as letting them win—whoever "they" are.

I had to stay to protect Fireside. Without me around, Jasper would be free to sponge any one of Mr. Pelton's horses. Even though I don't take too kindly to Mr. Pelton and his fat-cat ways, I've grown close to Fireside and the other horses in the stable, not to mention the boys. Someone's got to stick around to protect them.

Also, leaving now would make everyone think I didn't have the chibs to be a jockey. It's just like my buddy, Snapper, from back home said. Once you put your toe in that cold lake and show people you want to go in, you'd better end up swimming. Otherwise, everyone'll know you're chicken. Anyhow, the thought of stopping now . . . Hell, I'd sooner follow Showboat under a horse's stomping hooves.

So, I did what any bug boy would do: I weighed in and saddled up. Mr. Hodge gave me a plan for Lucky Chance, but it was as good as garbage once the bell rang. Majestic Tiger, the number three horse and the favorite, threw a shoe when he broke from the gate. His jockey, Mealy Russell, had to pull him up. That left me sitting second, right behind Little Eliza. Mr. Hodge hadn't even mentioned Little Eliza. It was only a six-furlong race, so I knew I had to make something happen sooner rather than later. I gave three taps with my whip and let Lucky have all the reins he wanted. I pulled to the inside and nosed in along the lead horse's flank. Toward the end of the backstretch, I managed to come up alongside Little Eliza's withers, a third of a length off the lead, which was perfect because it would force Eliza to the outside and make her run a wider turn. In a short race like this, running a wide turn is just about the worst thing you can do.

You always hear stories about jockeys coming up with clever ideas during races, performing feats of daring and defying the odds to win a race. I wish I had a story like that. I had exercised Lucky Chance no less than a hundred times, and he had never done anything to surprise me. He had never done anything to let me know he was better than middle-of-the-road. But, when he saw that open track ahead of him—all that freshly groomed dirt waiting to be eaten up—he reached out farther than I've ever seen a horse reach out. Every stride was longer than the last until we were two, three, four lengths out in the lead. It wasn't even close. I sent a field of seven other horses home without dessert—heck, those horses didn't even have a chance to start their salads by the time I was crossing the finish line.

For a bug boy to come in the money in his first two races— that ain't so bad. Hell, it's pretty damn good. No one expected Lucky Chance to come close, so all the credit went to me, Jack Walsh, the guy people were already calling the rising star of Pelton Stables. I sat in the winner's circle on top of Lucky Chance with Mr. Pelton, Mr. Hodge, and around a thousand people I'd never met before.

Still, there was no sign of Elizabeth, not even up there in her father's box.

Mr. Pelton had all sorts of nice things to say to me, but I didn't hear a word of it. He slipped me my ten-dollar bonus, and I just jammed it in my pocket. All I could focus on was that smile plastered across Mr. Hodge's face and that hand he was clapping on my back. That and all the flashbulbs popping.

A knock sounds on the stable door. *Jasper?* My breath goes still and I look for a place to hide. If it's him, I have nowhere to go. Although if it were him, I doubt he'd bother knocking. I roll off the cot and slink across the floor. I peek between the slats, ready to leap back if that thug smashes through the door.

I see ripped, ratty trousers and dusty boots. I see brass keys hanging from a belt loop. Bucky.

"I'm sleeping," I say. "Come back later."

"For Christ's sake, you got a girl in there or something?"

"Go be stupid someplace else."

"I got rid of Spoons," he whispers.

"You what?"

"I said I got rid of Spoons."

"He was my *pet*," I say. "We should have buried him."

"What was I supposed to do, sit him up at the card table in the jockeys' lounge until you got back? That monkey's dead and there ain't nothing we can do about it. So I got rid of him."

The thought of Bucky wrapping Spoons in old racing forms and tossing him into a waste bin in the picnic area pops into my mind. "What did you do with him?"

"Let me in and I'll tell you."

I unlatch the door and sit on my cot. Bucky swings the door wide, and daylight lances my eyeballs. "So what'd you do with him?"

"That ain't none of your concern," he says. "I just told you I'd tell you so you'd let me in."

"Spoons deserves a decent burial. What did you do with him?"

"All you need to know is I took care of it. Your job is to win races, Jack. You let me worry about dead monkeys and such. I'm your valet."

I heave my legs onto the cot and lie back down.

Bucky sits next to me. "You should hear the buzz about you on the grounds."

"What buzz?"

"You're all the talk down trackside. A bug boy coming in the money his first two times out? A bug boy winning his second race on a no-chancer? You're a hot piece of real estate, Jack. We have to line you up some freelance gigs before the magic wears off."

"We can't line anything up," I say. "We don't even know what horses I'm riding for Pelton yet. This week, next week, everything is up in the air." The truth is I have no faith that any of this will last. I'm all but a hundred percent sure that by tomorrow morning I'll be back mucking stalls and breezing ponies for five bucks a week.

"Problem solved." Bucky holds up a slip of paper. "Mr. Hodge gave this to me before I came down here."

I squint to see in the darkness of the stall and make out a dozen or so of Pelton's horses with a date and a number scrawled next to each one.

"Hodge tells me these are the horses you'll be riding," he says. "It's as far out as he's got figured. It's most of the meet as far as I can tell. He says you can ride whatever you want for any of the other races. You know, freelance. He's got a few mounts he wants you to breeze too, mostly ponies you'll be racing so you can get a feel for them, but nothing that won't take much time. He said he already spoke to you about that."

I nod.

"He also says not to get hurt."

Again I try to push Showboat from my mind and nod. I take the list from Bucky and run my eyes down the column of names. Some horses are better than others, and I notice Mr. Hodge has me riding Fireside three Wednesdays out in the Bolton Stakes. It's a big race. A twinge of excitement rises in my chest, but then I think of Jasper and the yellow sponge. That makes me think of Spoons and his death grimace. My heart hammers at the inside of my chest.

"Where are the other guys?" I say. "Where is Oatmeal? Where's Pug?"

"Them guys? They're out along the backstretch talking to reporters. They said they wanted to give those sportswriters something to sink their teeth into. The press is going crazy. They need something to put in the papers tomorrow, but you just up and disappeared!"

"Look," I say. "I've got to get some shut-eye. Get those guys away from the reporters. I don't want them saying anything dumb, and it just so happens that's what they're best at. We'll go out for dinner later on. It's on me."

"Where should I tell them guys we're going?"

"Shove off," I say. "Let me worry about that. You rustle up the boys and get them away from those newshounds."

"Yes, sir!" Like the best of valets, I suppose, Bucky does as I ask and disappears out the barn door. Seconds later, his head pokes back in. "Hey," he says. "You given any more thought to what we talked about in the doctor's office, you know, that thing with the sponge?" He points at his nostril.

"There's nothing to think about," I say. "Ain't gonna do it."

"But two hundred smackeroos . . ."

"No way. No how."

"You're the boss," Bucky says. "Oh, I almost forgot to mention, there's another filly on the back of that sheet I gave you. She was a late addition."

"A late addition?"

"You heard me."

I flip over the paper and there, right on the newsprint, is a set of bright red lip prints. A note just above it reads:

Jack,

I'm staying at the Adelphi Hotel. Pick me up at 7:00.

Don't be late.

Elizabeth

"Damn, she's sassy," I say.

"You like them that way and you know it," Bucky says. "And don't you try to jimmy your way out of dinner with us. A promise is a promise."

16

BUCKY WAS RIGHT. A PROMISE *IS* A PROMISE, BUT WITH the boys trailing behind me, I know how that Pied Piper guy must have felt when he led all those rats around. And the Adelphi Hotel is the last place anyone would want to lead rats. It's one of the fanciest hotels in Saratoga. The lounge is famous for real classy afternoon teas and supercolossal business deals. Only the highest of high society stays there. Only the fattest of the fat cats.

"Jack!" Oatmeal calls to me. "Wait up."

"Yeah," Bucky says. "You have to straighten these dunces out." He scurries up alongside me, his keys jingling. I can't help but notice that his left shoe has a hole near his big toe. His worn gray sock is poking through, and his toe is poking through that. "We've got a little bet going, the boys and me."

"When *don't* you have a little bet going?"

"Yeah, well, anyway," Bucky says. "Who would you say is the best horse in the history of horse racing?"

"The best horse in history?" I say.

"You heard him," Oatmeal says with a nod. "What horse was the best? You know, all-around best."

Pug comes up on my other side. "Hands down, it's Man o' War," he says. "It's got to be. You can't argue with that win percentage. In two seasons he went twenty for twenty-one. In his second season he went eleven for eleven. In one race, they gave him a hundred-and-thirty-eight-pound impost, and in another he won by a hundred lengths!"

"Don't try to sway him," Oatmeal says. "Man o' War didn't win the Triple Crown like Gallant Fox. And Man o' War doesn't come close to Gallant Fox's one-year earning record of three hundred and eight grand."

"That's because Man o' War raced fifteen years ago," Pug says. "Purses were smaller back in those days."

"Why do you guys have to ask me this right before we get to Elizabeth's hotel?" I step into the street and begin across Broadway. Of course, the boys follow, still a few paces back. Several cars skid to a stop, and horns start honking.

Bucky ignores them. "I don't know," he calls after me. "It's just what we were talking about. Before I knew it, they had a wager going. So, what do you think?"

"People don't consider the overseas stuff," I say. "There was one horse, Kinscem, from Hungary. It went unbeaten in fifty-four races. Best win-lose percentage ever. Then there's Logan. He was foaled in 1888 and ran three hundred and eighty-eight races. Three hundred and eighty-eight! And he won seventy-six of them. Another horse named Kingston made seventy-four starts and never once finished out of the money. Incredible."

"Hungary?" Pug says. "Hungary doesn't count."

"Just because it happens on dirt that'll never touch your

boots doesn't make it any less incredible," I say. "You asked what I thought and I told you. The truth is I have more interesting things on my mind."

"More interesting than the best horse of all time?" Pug says doubtfully.

I spin around to face them, all three of them. "I don't see any of you guys taking a girl out to dinner."

"All right, all right," Oatmeal says. "You don't have to get all frothed up about it, Jack. It was just a question."

"And all I'm saying is that you guys should try and think about the world beyond what's right in front of your noses."

Bucky, Oatmeal, and Pug glance at each other.

"So who wins the quarter?" Oatmeal asks.

As I look up, the rest of their banter drops away. I'm there. The dark-painted brick Adelphi stands in front of me. Above the front entrance, a second-story terrace as wide as the building looks out over Broadway. Even with the bustling goings-on of the street, I can hear some kind of violin music coming from up there, along with the unmistakable sounds of silver scraping against expensive plates and crystal glasses clinking. From the terrace, white columns rise another three stories to a roof decorated with yellow stonework that makes the building look like some kind of fancy wedding cake.

"Watch it," Pug whispers to the other guys. "We're getting dangerously close to the den of the fat cats."

"We should have brought pith helmets and hunting rifles," Oatmeal says. "We could have bagged us one, stuffed it, and brought it with us from track to track."

"Yeah, like a trophy," Pug adds.

I tell them to keep it down and wonder whether I should

just walk in the front door. The Adelphi seems like a place I shouldn't go into, and the expression on the doorman's face tells me I'm right.

"Hey there, Jack!" Elizabeth's voice is finer than the violins. She sounds close, but I can't see her anywhere. I look behind a few of the shrubs along the sidewalk, but I know she's not the type to lie behind a hedge, even on a lark. "Up here," the voice says.

Of course.

I look up and see her leaning over the railing of the veranda. She waves to me with her half-empty glass. "I'll be right down."

She's downstairs and outside before I have a chance to remind the guys about how they promised to scram when we got to the hotel, but when Elizabeth comes out, a dark cloth bundle tucked under her arm, they're nowhere to be found.

"I was starting to wonder if you got my note," she says. "It's almost eight. Don't you know better than to keep a lady waiting?"

"I—I—" I think about the lip prints on the paper, and wherever the guys scrammed to, I hope they stay scrammed. "Sorry. I fell asleep," I say. "It's been a tough few days."

She runs a gloved hand along my shoulder. "Let's see what we can do to get you to unwind."

Elizabeth tosses her bundle into the open top of a Bugatti parked in front of the hotel and unlatches the passenger door. "After you," she says.

I know better than to let a gal open a door for me, but before I can protest, she says, "Let's not waste time with pretenses. Just get in. Dinner, right?"

"This is *your* Bugatti?" I manage to say.

She holds a key in front of my nose and jingles it back and forth.

I slip into the car and sink into the yellow leather upholstery. The seat wraps around my body like it was built just for me. Elizabeth walks around the front and gets in the driver's seat. "Where to?" she says.

I grabbed all the money I had stashed away. With the five dollars Mr. Hodge gave me and the sawbuck from Mr. Pelton for today's win, I managed to put together $19.35. I never go out for dinner, so I have no idea what it costs. Most nights I scrounge for leftovers at the commissary of whatever track we happen to be at. But, if Elizabeth's family owns a Bugatti, if her family has a box next to Mr. Pelton at the track, she's probably used to the best of the best. Even with the boys gone, I know I'm going to come up short.

"I have an idea," Elizabeth says. She starts the car and wiggles the shifter. Finally, she finds the slot and shoves the stick forward. The engine squeals. The car shudders. Then, it dies out. "I do that all the time," she says, smiling.

I want to offer to drive for her. It would be the gentlemanly thing to do. Anyway, driving this car might be more exciting than winning *ten* races at the track. I've driven Mr. Hodge's truck on errands countless times, but I can't bring myself to offer to get behind the wheel of this beauty. It's one thing for Elizabeth to grind the gears, but if I did it I'd probably drop dead.

Elizabeth starts the Bugatti again and shifts it into gear. The engine growls, and this time the car lurches out onto Broadway. It sputters and almost stalls, but Elizabeth gives it some more gas and the car coughs back to life. "I'm terrible with these things," she says. "My uncle taught me to drive on holiday at his estate on Long Island, but I never saw much use. Living in Manhattan doesn't afford me many opportunities for practice. Hey, grab that bundle there."

Every time she grinds the gears, my shoulders tighten. This car costs more than I'm likely to make my whole life, and Elizabeth is treating it worse than I would an old, unmatched shoe. The bundle is heavier than I expected.

"Congratulations on your second race, by the way."

"Thanks," I say.

"That was quite an upset you pulled there. Cost me a few dollars, that's for sure."

"Sorry." I run a finger along the edge of the door. The chrome sparkles in the setting sun. "It might have turned out different if Majestic Tiger actually made it out of the gate."

"Don't sell yourself short," she says. "Eliza is no slouch. And with Linus McCready on her back, I thought for sure she would win. Daddy was upset, that being one of his favorite ponies. We picked her up at the auctions here two years ago. She was the first one I helped him with, and she's got quite a good record."

"Little Eliza is yours?"

"Where do you think the name came from?"

Eliza. Elizabeth. It's so obvious.

"I'm sorry, I—"

"Don't be, Jack. You raced brilliantly. You're the talk of the town. At least you are until some other jockey does something to top you. And lucky me. I have you all to myself." She reaches across and touches my knee, but her hand leaves just as quickly when she needs to shift again. The Bugatti bucks.

I look down at the bundle in my hands. It's a blue knitted

shawl wrapped around something. Something cool. Something square. Something filled with liquid.

"Unwrap it, you lunkhead," Elizabeth says.

I peel back the cloth folds and find a crystal bottle filled with golden fluid. "Where'd you get the whiskey?" I ask.

"In case you haven't heard, Prohibition's over. Whiskey is everywhere. It's like someone had it all piled up at the border waiting for the laws to change. Once they did, the bars were stocked and the barkeeps were pouring before the ink on the paperwork dried."

"I know that, but where did you get it?"

"I nipped it from the bar in our hotel room."

I uncork the bottle. Even with the wind rushing past us, the smell of whiskey burns my nose. The boys make their own rotgut by mixing apple juice and sugar in a mason jar and leaving it to sit in the barn for a few weeks, but I never touch that stuff. I've heard stories of homemade booze blinding folks. As for this, it doesn't smell half bad.

"Give it here," a voice that is not Elizabeth's says. A hand reaches over my shoulder and snatches the bottle away from me. It's Bucky.

Elizabeth laughs.

"What the hell are you doing here?" I say.

Bucky takes a swig from the bottle. "You wanted us to make ourselves scarce, and there weren't no place to go but into the Bugatti."

"Us?" I say.

Oatmeal's head pops up next to Bucky's. "We needed *someplace* to hide," he says. He grabs the bottle away from Bucky and takes a slug. "All three of us."

"All three of you?"

Pug's head pops up between the other two. "I told you this is a fat-cat car!" he cries out.

I glance at Elizabeth to see if she gets cross at Pug for calling her a fat cat. She just laughs.

Bucky taps me on the shoulder. "So where are we headed?"

"We?" I say.

"You said you'd take us out tonight, and a promise is a promise."

"It's true," Elizabeth says. "A promise *is* a promise."

My hands grip my threadbare trouser legs so tightly I think my nails might tear right through. I want nothing more than to ditch the guys and have Elizabeth all to myself.

"I have an idea," Oatmeal says. "Why don't we start by picking up a few of your girlfriends, Elizabeth?"

"I have a better idea," she says. "Let's head to the park and work on that bottle you've got there."

The boys pass the bottle around the backseat as though they're trying to finish it before we get there. The Bugatti, with Elizabeth behind the wheel, coughs and sputters its way down Broadway. We head straight out of town and into the country, away from the bustling hotels and restaurants, away from the moving picture theaters. We head toward the darkness of the lengthening shadows. Toward the Saratoga Reservation—toward the construction site for Roosevelt's Saratoga spa complex.

17

I DIDN'T SEE YOU IN THE PADDOCK AFTER MY FIRST race," I say to Elizabeth.

We're sitting apart from the boys at the shallow end of the newly completed Victoria Pool. From what I've heard, it's going to be the first outdoor heated pool in the country, and judging from the brick archways and marble columns surrounding it, there's no doubt it'll be the nicest one for a long time. Although it's already dark, the bluestone patio is still warm from the long day in the sun. Our shoes are off and Elizabeth has pulled her dress up to her thighs as our feet dangle into the cool water. It's not at all proper or ladylike, and it makes me like her more.

"I know I was sort of swept up, what with all the photographs and champagne in the winner's circle," I say, "but I figured you might—"

"I don't wait on jockeys," Elizabeth says. "What do you take me for, some kind of autograph hound?" She says it in a playful sort of way, but her words still bite a little.

"But you're so good at telling me how I'm *not* a jockey."

"I don't wait on bug boys either." She leans back and rests on her elbows. The moon makes her hair glow almost blue, and I turn so I can see her better.

Bucky, Oatmeal, and Pug are horsing around at the deep end. They are stripped down to their Skivvies and taking turns jumping into the pool and passing the bottle around. They've managed to get through a good amount of Elizabeth's bourbon and are showing no signs of being bashful as they cavort half-naked in front of a girl.

"Guys," I call over to them in a hushed sort of way. "Keep it down. The cops might find us." Then I remember hearing about an encampment back here for homeless, unattached men who are helping with landscaping and building walls, benches, and railings. "Or one of the landscapers from the transient camp," I add.

"And save some of that bourbon for us," Elizabeth adds. "That's top-shelf stuff."

"Sure thing, little missy," Bucky says as he tilts the bottle back and takes a gulp. His foot slips on the bluestone and he falls backward into a lounge chair. He holds the crystal bottle aloft, triumphant that he didn't shatter it on the patio. Oatmeal and Pug giggle like they've just seen the funniest thing in the world.

I put my feet next to Elizabeth's. Hers make mine look like baby feet. "So, how did you do at the track today?" I ask.

"As good a day as any, I suppose."

"Super."

"That upset you pulled, though. It sure did cut into my numbers. I had you at thirty to one. More than a few of my girls put money on that horse of yours, Jack."

"Sorry about that," I say, a little irritated she only had me at thirty to one.

"I suppose that's all part of the business." Elizabeth splashes me with her foot and turns to me. "But tell me: how did you do it? How did you pull it out against my Eliza?"

I don't want to tell her I have no idea where Lucky Chance's speed came from. I want her to think I had something to do with it. "I just rode her harder than I've ever rode her before," I say. "I took her through her paces and did what Mr. Hodge told me to do."

"Well, you could've given me a little heads-up." Her shoulders hunch, and I can't help but wonder if she's doing nearly as well with her bookmaking business as she's letting on.

"So, what's there to do around here?" I ask, hoping to steer the conversation to anything but horse racing.

"I thought you'd been to Saratoga before."

"I have," I say. "It's just the first time I've been to Saratoga at night. You know, the first time I've gone out in Saratoga at night to enjoy myself."

"How could you come to Saratoga and not go out on the town? Aside from the track, it's the only thing decent people do around here."

I want to remind her what I do for a living, at least what I did until today. I want her to understand that going out until all hours of the morning might be what rich folks on summer holiday do, but it's not what stableboys do—not ones who want to keep their jobs anyway. We have to be up and ready at four in the morning and work most of the day in the heat, while her kind gets to sit in the shade sipping lemonade. But I don't say those things. It's not her fault what I do or what family she was born into.

"I guess I never really had the clothes to go out," I say, looking down at my rags, my worn-out trousers rolled up to my knees. I couldn't bring myself to put on Showboat's blazer again after what happened to him. "I guess I never really had the clothes *or* the money."

"We'll have to see what we can do about that," Elizabeth says. She digs in her purse and pulls out a crisp stack of bills. She peels a few off and shoves them in my hand.

I look down and see I'm holding a fistful of tens and twenties. She's given me no less than a hundred bucks. "I can't take this from you," I say.

"Who says I'm giving you anything? It's a loan. Pay me back when you're able. If it makes you feel any better, I'll charge you interest—a point a day. I know it's steep, but try to find anything better in Saratoga Springs during track season." Elizabeth gets up and makes her way around the pool, weaving between lounge chairs, tables, and work equipment until she gets to the boys. She takes the bottle from Oatmeal and sucks down a healthy swig. "Give these guys some cash, Jack. Let's go someplace nice. I want you to take me out on the town."

She leaps over a low fence and begins to run barefoot across the grass toward the car. With her arms spread out and her dress billowing, she looks like some sort of magical fairy.

I make my way over to the boys, and Bucky gives me a wink. "I think we'll be fine right here," he says. He raises the bottle. "Right here with our bottle of hooch and the ten dollars you're about to give us."

"Ten dollars?"

Bucky shrugs. "You've got to do something to make up for

the promise you're about to break. Anyhow, the boys and I want to catch a flick in town."

I start flipping through my bills. "You sure? It's a long walk."

He nods. "Sure, I'm sure—we'll hoof it—so long as you give me all the juicy details tomorrow, chum."

I hand Bucky a ten.

"For another five I'll give you a juicy piece of advice."

I dig in my pocket and drop a five in Bucky's lap.

He snaps it up and folds the money in half. "Put on your shoes and roll down your pants legs. You look ridiculous."

I go to grab my money back, but Bucky already has it tucked away. I put on my shoes and roll down my pants legs just like he told me. Then I chase after Elizabeth.

"If things don't work out with you two . . . ," Oatmeal calls after me.

"Shut up," I say over my shoulder.

"I've got a thing for taller women!"

"Didn't you hear the guy?" Pug says. "He said to shut up. You better listen to Jack. He's our new gravy train."

"*New* gravy train?" Bucky says, his voice now faint in the distance. "I didn't know we had an *old* gravy train!"

When Elizabeth and I get to the car, she tosses me the keys. I look at the Bugatti as if it's a holy relic. It's one of the top cars in the world, and I'm about to get behind the wheel. All the driving I've done in Mr. Hodge's truck seems like nothing.

I let Elizabeth in and shut her door carefully, as if slamming it could spoil the perfect balance of the engine. I make my way around to the driver's side and get in. The car starts on the first try, and I coax her into gear. She sounds like a purring lion as we accelerate down the side streets. I have to swerve hard a few times to avoid ruts and holes in the road, but before long I get used to how she handles.

"How do you like driving a fat-cat car?" Elizabeth says.

I glance at her. Her bare feet are propped on the dashboard, and her hair flows back over the headrest.

"I could get used to this," I say.

"You could get used to being a fat cat?"

"No, but I could get used to driving a fat-cat car. There's a difference."

"Fair enough," she says. "Hey, make a left here. Go up there." Elizabeth directs me through the city a few times, up and down Broadway, on the streets that wind around the racetrack, and in and out of countless back roads. Finally, she directs me straight out Church Street a few miles until we come upon a huge mansion on our right—or at least what looks like a huge mansion.

"There's the Brook," she says. "Pull up there."

The thought of going into the Brook is scarier than going into the Adelphi a dozen times over wearing a burlap sack for a shirt and feed bags on my feet. The Brook is the ritziest place in the city. It used to be owned by Arnold Rothstein. Yes, *that* Arnold Rothstein, the guy who fixed the 1919 World Series. I remember reading about this place once. Rothstein said, "People like to think they're better than other people and as long as they're willing to pay to prove it, I'm willing to let them."

He was right.

The Brook is where the richest people go. I've seen it in the social pages, but I never imagined I'd be coming here. Sophie Tucker and Helen Morgan perform here. Marlene Dietrich and all the other movie stars come here. I've even heard that Lucky Luciano, Joe Adonis, and lots of other gangsters come here.

I glance down at my clothes. "Elizabeth, I don't think—"

"Hush up and pull in," she says. "You agreed to take me out to dinner, and this is where I'd like to go."

I pull up to the gate, where two uniformed Saratoga policemen motion for me to stop. Behind them, on the balcony of the main building, two men in dark suits and fedoras stare down at us. In the uplights of the entranceway, I can see they're holding machine guns. "Where do you think you're going?" the officer closer to me says. "Aren't you out a bit late for a kid your age?"

Elizabeth leans across and hugs my shoulder. "I'm Jim Reed's girl," she says. "My father comes here all the time. We're just headed up for a bite to eat."

The two rows of brass buttons on each of their uniforms gleam in my headlights like twin V-shaped constellations. The officer nearer to me looks at the other and nods.

"Very good," the other officer says to Elizabeth like I'm not even there. "But I doubt you'll get past Pietro, not with a guy dressed as shabby as that." He opens the gate, and they allow us to pass.

I drive the car to the awning that leads up the stairs. One of the valets rushes to the Bugatti. It's the only cream-colored car in a sea of black ones, and it's plain to see everyone knows who owns it.

"Miss Reed," the valet says as he opens her door. "It is such a pleasure to see you again." He looks across the seat at me, and his expression changes from pleasant to just-stepped-in-horse-manure-with-his-new-shoes. He clears his throat. "And you are . . . ?"

"Ummm."

"This is Jack Walsh," Elizabeth says, squeezing my arm. "He's the newest and best jockey with Pelton Stables. And he is my escort tonight."

"I see," the valet says.

Elizabeth goes on. "You might have heard about his big win over Majestic Tiger and Little Eliza in the fifth, and it would do you well to run along and find him a proper jacket to wear. His tuxedo is being cleaned." She stuffs a bill into the man's hand.

The valet gives her a smile. "But of course."

I get out of the car, and flashbulbs start popping. Reporters from all the papers are here and they start calling for our attention. Of course, they know Elizabeth's name, but I'm surprised to discover some of them know mine as well. I turn around a few times, unsure what I should do, and the flashbulbs pop even faster. Tiny white circles fill my vision. A hand grabs me by the wrist, and Elizabeth guides me up the stairs and through the front door. She pulls me from the lavish lobby, appointed with huge carved armchairs, into an office where the valet is waiting with a suit on a hanger and a pair of shiny black shoes.

"I hope these will do," he says, hanging the suit on a hook on the back of the door.

"They'll do splendidly," Elizabeth says. She hands him another bill. "Thank you, Pietro."

"If you need a different size—"

"They'll be fine."

After the valet leaves, Elizabeth turns her back. "Get on with it, then," she says. "I don't have all night."

I toss my old clothes in the corner and put on the borrowed suit and shoes. Everything fits well, and I wonder if the valet works days in a haberdashery. Pietro nailed my size like I can nail a half mile in forty-eight and a fifth. The fine cotton of the shirt feels so much nicer than the coarse fabric I'm used to.

By the time Elizabeth turns around, I'm fumbling with my tie. "Here, let me help," she says. "I tie my father's for him all the time." She loops and twists and folds the striped silk until I feel it cinch lightly around my neck.

Elizabeth steps back and smiles.

I button my jacket. "How do I look?"

"You look magnificent," she says. "You look magnificent, except . . ."

"Except what?"

She points at my face and her eyebrows squeeze together. "You have lipstick on your cheek."

"What?" My fingers start wiping frantically. "I don't have lipstick on my cheek."

"Sure you do," she says. "Right there."

I wipe some more. "Did I get it off?"

"Let me see." She steps closer and plants a kiss right where she had been pointing. Her lips feel softer than the tip of a foal's ear. "Nope, you didn't get it. In fact, it looks a little darker now."

She's so close I can feel the heat coming off her body, like off the withers of a freshly breezed mare. "Maybe you could balance it out," I say. I turn my other cheek toward her. "You know, plant one on the other side."

She does. This kiss feels even softer than the first.

"How about here?" she whispers. She takes my face in her hands and pulls my mouth to hers. I can still taste the whiskey

on her lips, but if whiskey tasted this sweet, I'd have to support Prohibition. No one would ever get anything done and
we'd all die drunk in the gutter. I push up on my toes to meet
her, to get more. She responds by pulling me closer.

At first I think it's my heart pounding, but then I realize
someone's knocking on the door.

"Ignore it," Elizabeth whispers in my ear.

I glance over and see there's no lock. If whoever's knocking wants to come in, there's no stopping them. I pull away
from Elizabeth and wipe my face with my handkerchief.

I only open the door halfway so as to give Elizabeth a
chance to compose herself. It's Pietro, the valet. He looks at
me from nose to tail. "My goodness, quite a transformation."

"Thank you, Pietro," I say. "We'll be right out."

"Very good, sir. You should know there's a gentleman asking for you at the maître d' stand."

"For me?"

He nods. "He's an odd fellow with an ample paunch. His
shoes don't match his belt. In any case, he insists he knows
you, and he says it's urgent."

None of the boys have paunches. Neither does Mr. Hodge.
Mr. Pelton has a big belly, but I'd bet everything in my
pocket—even the money Elizabeth lent me that I'm paying a
point a day on—that the valet knows Mr. Pelton's name. Even
if he didn't, I doubt anyone would describe Mr. Pelton as
"odd." Jasper doesn't have a big belly either. My father comes
to mind, but he's built like a log cabin. He's not the kind of
guy you'd think of as having an "ample paunch."

"Did you get his name?" I ask.

"Yes, sir," Pietro says. "He told me his name is Tweed.
Tweed McGowan."

18

"You're looking fine, m'boy!" Tweed ruffles my hair like I'm still twelve years old—like he still has the right to put his grimy hands on me. "So much like your father, y'are."

He motions for me to sit next to him at the bar. It's a tight squeeze on account of the Brook being packed full of people, and I don't want to get that close to him. If anything has changed about Tweed, it's that he's gotten fatter. Fatter and more disgusting. When the valet said the man had an "ample paunch," he was being polite. Tweed's shirt looks stuffed to bursting, like each button is struggling to stay attached to the fabric. His neck bulges from his collar and leads up to a face that's redder than a McIntosh in late October.

Tweed angles the only empty stool in the place toward me. "Grab some wood, son."

I push my hair back into place and slide the barstool against the bar with my foot. "Thanks," I say, "but I'd rather stand." I glance around and find Elizabeth. She's hobnobbing with an older man and two women over the rich sounds of the orchestra. Several girls, one who I recognize as her runner, Jane, stand at her side. Elizabeth's eyes meet mine, and she flashes me a smile.

"Come on," Tweed says. He holds his arm out as though if I sit down it might creep around me. "Take a load off."

I fold my arms across my chest and rest a shiny wingtip on the footrest of the barstool, pinning it against the bar.

"Suit yourself. Suit yourself." Tweed knocks back the rest of his drink and motions the bartender for another. The tuxedoed bartender selects a bottle from among the hundreds that stand on narrow shelves against the smoky mirror. When he arrives with the bottle, Tweed snatches it from his hand and reaches across the bar for another glass. "We'll take the whole thing," he says, setting the glass in front of me. "Let me buy you a drink, Jack."

After they stopped with all that Prohibition nonsense last year, drinking age was set at eighteen. Sure, I'm more than two years shy, but here in Saratoga no one cares. The rule is to keep the folks who spend money happy. And jockeys spend money. Heaps of it. Even so, I have no interest in having a drink with this bastard.

"No, thanks," I say. "I'm watching my weight."

He nods a few times. "So, how's your family doing? Your mom, your dad, and that little Penelope? What's her name again?"

"Penny," I say.

"Right, right. Penny."

"Fine, as far as I know," I say. "I hear my dad's down in Albany looking for work. No news is good news, I suppose."

"These days that's too true," Tweed says. He raises his glass and takes a sip. "Sure do wish you'd have one with me, though. I guess I'll have to drink for two." He pours himself another and knocks it back in one shot. "Anyway, how have you been?"

How have I been? This is the guy that beat the stitches out of me every night with a riding crop. This is the guy that did so much worse when he got really looped on backwoods moonshine. After he started thinking I wasn't worth the air I was breathing, this is the guy that traded me to Pelton Stables for an old saddle and some horseshoes. *Good riddance to bad garbage,* he said as I gathered my things and hopped into Mr. Hodge's late-model Ford truck.

I shrug.

"Come on," Tweed says. "There must be something going on."

It occurs to me that this is no coincidence. He wants something from me. "Things are looking up," I say.

"Is that right?" He's playing stupid—pretending he doesn't know about my promotion—like everyone in the whole town doesn't already know.

Tweed pours himself another and scoops it up. Booze sloshes over the rim onto his hand. He drains half the glass in one gulp and faces me. "All right," he says. "Let's cut to the chase here. I've never been one to mince words. I've decided on a little change in career, m'boy, and it just so happens that I think we can help each other."

"We can help each other?"

"Sure can. I'm going to cut to the chase here."

"You already said that," I say. "So start cutting."

"All right then." Tweed jingles the ice in his glass and takes another swig. "The truth is I saw you race today and think you have some potential. I'm not saying you've got what it takes to be a top jockey or anything, but it just so happens I'm an agent now. We can be a team. I'll line up the rides, and you can win 'em. We'll split the profits—half for you, half for me."

"Agents only take ten percent," I say.

"Numbers are always negotiable, m'boy." Tweed swings his arm wildly. It's a miracle he doesn't clobber someone. What's left of his drink spills from his glass, some on the sleeve of his jacket and the rest down the front of his pants.

I back away. "Thanks for the offer," I say, "but—"

"But nothing," Tweed says. He heaves himself from his barstool and staggers toward me. He stabs his sausage finger at me. "If it wasn't for me, you wouldn't be here. You'd still be rolling around in the dirt on that sorry excuse for a farm. I gave you horse racing." He swings his arm again. Ice cubes fly from his drink and skitter across the bar. "I gave you everything!"

A few heads turn to watch, but between the commotion of the drinkers and the din of the orchestra, not many people seem to notice.

Tweed staggers closer, and I back away some more. Elizabeth is nowhere to be seen. She and the girls have disappeared. I back away farther—as much as I can in the tightly packed bar—but Tweed comes at me, this time with anger painted all over his ugly mug.

"I brought you into this business!" His glass drops from his hand and shatters on the floor. "You owe me. I cul-cul-cultivated you!"

Suddenly, a shriek rings out next to me. It's Jane, and she's pointing at Tweed. "How dare you!" she hollers. She smacks Tweed across the face. "How dare you be so, so, so . . . disrespectful!" She smacks him again.

The bar goes quiet. The band stops playing. I can see Pietro making his way through the crowd to where we're standing, but Jane goes on. "I'm not some kind of harlot—some kind of floozy—you can just have your way with!" she says. "What kind of girl do you think I am?"

"I-I-I—" Tweed sputters, but he can't seem to get anything more past his bloated lips.

"Is there any trouble, ma'am?" Pietro says.

"I'll say there's trouble," Jane says. "This sorry excuse for a man grabbed my . . . my . . ." She moves her gloved hands around her torso in circles, not really pointing to any spot exactly. Then, she spins on Pietro and plants her fists on her hips. "What kind of place are you running here?"

"I'm terribly sorry," he says. "I will have this gentleman removed immediately."

"I should think so," Jane says, spitting each word from her mouth. "But please refrain from calling him gentle . . . or a man. He's nothing but a fat, disgusting worm!"

A chuckle spreads through the crowd.

Tweed tries to say something, but Pietro shoots him a look sterner than a preacher staring down a noisy kid during Sunday church services. He steps between Jane and Tweed as two gorillas in tuxedos turn up and stand on either side of him. "You have two choices," Pietro says to Tweed in a low yet dead serious voice. "You can leave amiably, or we can see that you and your cheap blazer are removed. Either way, your evening here is finished."

One of the tuxedoed men grabs Tweed's shoulder, but Tweed shakes the guy off. He slides off his stool, straightens his tie, and smoothes down his jacket where the bouncer's hand had been. His scarce and stringy blond hair sticks straight up, revealing a flaky, sunburned scalp. "I'll leave on my own, thank you," Tweed says. Then, he turns to me. "I'll see you later."

As soon as the bouncers get Tweed a safe distance away, the clamor and revelry start on up again. Within seconds, it's as if nothing happened.

"I must apologize, Miss Mooney," Pietro says to Jane. He calls the bartender over and orders us a round of drinks on the house. "I promise you this won't happen again."

"See that it doesn't," she says. "My father would be most disappointed."

A pinched smile spreads across his face. "Yes, well, I see no reason to get him involved. The situation is quite under control now."

"Thank you for your gallantry, Pietro."

He bows slightly. "No problem whatsoever," he says. "If you'd follow me, I have a table ready for you and your party. As the ladies have requested, it's just next to the dance floor."

"Thank you." Jane offers me her arm and leads me across the restaurant behind Pietro. It's the first time my eyes take in the ballroom, and it's simply huge. It looks too big for this mansion to contain. Massive, glittering chandeliers hang from a towering ceiling held up by twenty-foot columns. The room is surrounded by archways and doors that lead to various smaller parlors. The orchestra sits on a riser at one end opposite a glass-paned wall that leads to another huge room, a full casino with roulette, bird cages, and craps tables.

Jane is far more attractive without that hat covering most of her face. She wears her dark hair short and wavy, almost pasted to her head, and her huge blue eyes fill her face as though she was the original model for Betty Boop. When we get to the table, Elizabeth and a few other girls are already waiting.

I take the seat next to Elizabeth, and she squeezes my knee under the table. "I thought you might need a little help," she says.

"I could have handled it myself."

"I don't doubt it for a second," she says, "but let's say you slugged him and broke your hand. What would happen to your riding career?"

"Over nearly before it began."

Elizabeth nods. "Anyway, if you got into a scrape, they would have asked you to leave, and I do so love their beef Wellington."

Beef Wellington. I've heard of it, but I have no idea what it is. The thought of food makes me realize how hungry I am. I pull the slip of paper Bucky gave me from my pocket and see that I have to weigh in at 106 again tomorrow. I can't afford to gain weight. "So, you sent Jane to my rescue," I say.

Jane slides into the seat next to me. "You didn't think I was just around for my stunning looks, did you? Anyhow, it's good practice."

"Jane wants to go to Hollywood as soon as she turns eighteen," Elizabeth says. "She's better than a natural. She's going to reinvent what it means to be a movie star. Already, she has a few auditions lined up in the fall."

"Well, as far as I'm concerned, you deserve an Academy Award."

"Thanks," Jane says, "but that would have been for Best *Supporting* Actress, and I won't rest until I get Best Actress."

"Not that I needed any help, of course," I say.

"Of course," Elizabeth says, smiling. She smoothes her

napkin on her lap, and her hand works its way to my thigh. She squeezes higher than the last time.

We order our food. I decide on the chicken cordon bleu. When the waiter brings the first course, my stomach starts rumbling like it could leap out of me and eat the salad on its own. I know I shouldn't touch the food, but all I want to do is shove every last bit of it into my mouth. "Ladies," I say. "If you'll excuse me for a moment . . ."

I head to the bathroom and lean on the sink. I take a few deep breaths. The attendant smiles at me and nods. I gaze at the mirror. It's the first time I've looked at myself in one since dropping all my weight. My cheeks are hollow, and my bones look fragile through my thin skin. Like bird bones. My eyes seem larger than usual, and my lips are dry and cracked, probably from not drinking water for the past two days. In the borrowed suit, I look more like a guy who just got sprung from prison than a fifteen-year-old.

I wonder what I should do about eating. That plate is going to be sitting right in front of me, and I know I'll have no choice but to eat it. It would be rude not to eat it. Who am I kidding? I'm too hungry not to eat it. But gaining a single ounce is not an option. If I miss weight tomorrow, Mr. Hodge will probably yank a whole slew of my lower-impost rides. Even though I came in the money twice today, I'm still replaceable. My stomach tightens some more, and I wonder if I could get anything down at this point anyway.

A retching sound comes from behind me. Then another. The toilet flushes, and I see a smaller man back out of one of the stalls. A jockey. When he turns around, I recognize him. It's the guy who whipped me across the leg—the guy who was standing right there when Spoons dropped out of my locker.

He grins at me and claps me on the back. "Hey, no hard feelings about earlier today," he says. "You ran a great fifth. You've got some talent, kiddo."

"Thanks," I say.

"Better watch out tomorrow, though." He gives me a playful punch in the shoulder. "You won't catch me off guard again."

I want to be polite, but it's hard with a guy who not eight hours ago cost me a win in my first race.

He puts his hand on my shoulder and leans in so close I can smell the vomit on his breath. His teeth are the color of apple cores that got left out in the sun too long. "Hey, what was with that dead monkey, though?" he whispers to me. "Some kind of prank or something?"

In my mind I can see Spoons's upturned face, his jaw clenched. That vision will be burned there forever.

"No idea," I say.

"People do some damn crazy stuff when they're half-starved and desperate to win a race. Half those guys are in hock up to their eyebrows, and when a new guy comes along, well, they don't take too kindly to it. Welcome to professional horse racing, son."

"Some welcome."

"Anyhow, I better get back out there," he says. "I got a pair of fillies that need someone to butter their bread."

"Good luck," I say. I smile at him as he throws a handful of change into the attendant's cup and grabs a mint.

Halfway out the door, he turns around to face me. His tie is loose, and his top button is unbuttoned. "And remember," he says. He flips a thumb toward the bathroom stall. "If you're gonna binge, you'd better purge."

19

THE RINGING OF THE STARTING BELL SHAKES ME TO my toes. The doors slam open and Skee Ball breaks from the gate slower than sap. The rest of the field is busy at work while my horse is trotting along like he'd rather be sipping tea on the veranda at the Adelphi.

It's a slow day at the track, especially slow for a Saturday, most likely on account of the heat. The crowd doesn't give its usual roar, but for me this is a big race. It's my fourth day competing, but my first as a freelance rider.

I landed the mount yesterday morning after I breezed Fireside on special request for Mr. Hodge. It seems Slouch Halpern busted his arm when he got tossed by a nervous colt—bone came clear through the skin. They needed someone to ride Skee Ball on short notice, and that's where I came in. Even though I have to wear pink silks with yellow polka dots, I jumped at the opportunity. I stand to make a nice stack of cash if I take the win. Elizabeth explained the math to me last night, and we went over it until I got it straight.

It's a three-year-old allowance race with a twelve-hundred-dollar purse. An allowance race is usually reserved for promising horses, the up-and-comers. It's like the bush leagues in baseball, but instead of ballplayers looking at getting into the big leagues, it's for horses looking to get into a stakes race. A win here would not only earn Alberta Crest Stables, the stable I'm riding for, a shot at the big time but also get them sixty percent of that twelve-hundred-dollar purse, ten percent of which would go to me. Turns out that's seventy-two bucks for one race. Even placing or showing would earn me a nice payday — thirty percent or ten percent, the remainder of the purse, which comes out to thirty-six bucks or twelve bucks respectively.

The good news is that one of the conditions put on this race is that it's for horses who have not won a race since May 22, and Skee Ball's last win was on May 21. This means the racing secretary had Skee Ball in mind when he was putting this race together. I'm on the favored mount.

The bad news is Skee Ball. Skee Ball, a light gray gelding with a black mane who I exercised a few times as a favor back at Belmont, can be counted on for one thing and one thing only: to be completely unpredictable. Some days he's spot-on, and other days he's about as focused as a nervous canary. Today, with all the bucking and jerking he was doing during the post parade, I didn't have high hopes. Nervousness before a race is not a good sign. The best I can wish for is that once his heart starts pounding like a blast furnace, once he sees those other horses stretching out their leads, Skee Ball will turn all that jitter into skitter.

Skee Ball isn't one of those horses that likes being in the middle of the action, so he jerks to the right, away from the others, who are all clustered along the rail. I urge him into the fray with a tug of the reins. I brush him across his flank with my whip. Skee Ball begins to drift left—to focus on the race at hand.

As the grandstand gets farther and farther behind us, the sounds of the crowd fade. The jockeys chatter back and forth, but their words are swallowed up by the rumble of hooves and the wind rushing through my helmet. I urge Skee Ball on and stay pinned to the streaming tail in front of us. Although Skee Ball and I are taking a wider turn than most of the others, by the time we straighten out into the backstretch, there are only two horses ahead.

Tucker Lennon is riding Churchill Charlie. Tucker seems like a decent enough guy. He helped me with the sweatbox in the jockeys' lounge yesterday when I needed to drop a pound and a half on short notice. I wouldn't call Tucker a friend—I wouldn't call any of the jockeys my friend—but like I said, he seems a decent enough guy.

Gimpy Gamble is riding Pratfall. Gimpy was just hired on by Greenwillow Stables about a month ago. Word around the shed row is that Gimpy's ankle was crushed into gravel as he tried to save his brother from under a panicky stallion. According to Linus, Gimpy ain't been right in the head since the accident, and he races like all of us jockeys had a hand in stomping his brother to death.

Tucker and Gimpy are running side by side—a wall of horsemeat. The muscular hindquarters of their mounts ripple with every stride. Hooves pound earth, sending clumps of dirt into the air like shrapnel.

I sit third. I let the race happen and wait for my opening, but it doesn't come. Every time Tucker pulls away from the rail or Gimpy drifts a little wide, they close the gap back up before I have a chance to make my move. On most horses I'd see if something unfolds on the far turn or once we hit the homestretch, but Skee Ball isn't any closer. He needs to get his nose up in the action before the final turn. Anyhow, in a seven-furlong race, there ain't much time to sit back and wait for anything. It goes by in a minute and a half, give or take.

Tucker and Gimpy separate again. I know the gap isn't nearly large enough, but I take my shot. I urge Skee Ball between the two lead horses, and Pratfall gives way.

"Stay off my ass," Gimpy calls out to me.

I nudge Skee Ball ahead even more. Gimpy tries to shut the opening down by jerking his reins to the left, but Skee Ball finds the energy and pushes forward. Two other horses fill the space behind me. It's a tight race.

The announcer calls out something, and I can hear the crowd respond. Must be he's saying I'm making my move. Before I know it, we're three horses across and getting ready to enter the far turn.

"Son of a bitch!" Gimpy cries out.

Something grabs hold of my right heel and yanks. My balance turns upside down, and I can feel myself tumbling. It's Gimpy. He's grabbed my boot and is tossing me from my mount. It's the worst foul someone can pull—it could kill a guy. I think about the two horses that filled the gap behind me. I'm dead meat when I hit the ground.

I suck in a gasp. My hands flail around for something to grab on to. I can't catch hold of anything. I see Gimpy's sneer. I see the sky. I see Skee Ball's mane whipping in the wind. I'm falling to the left. My stomach lurches into my throat. I get ready for the six-foot fall and to go limp. I get ready for a twelve-hundred-pound Thoroughbred's hoof to pound into my chest or crush my skull.

A strong hand grabs hold of my jersey and tugs. I feel myself being lifted up, tossed back over my horse. It's Tucker. He's pulled me back onto Skee Ball.

"Get up there!" he shouts. "You looking to meet your Maker or something?"

Everything turns right side up again. I get my feet into the irons and squat over the saddle. I center my knees over my toes and lean forward.

Tucker saved me. He grabbed my silks and saved me midrace.

"Thanks!" I call out.

Tucker says nothing. I glance at him. His eyes are forward, concerned with the track ahead of him.

Gimpy's gained a half length on Tucker and me, and we've both lost speed. It takes a lot of a Thoroughbred's energy to get going again, but what choice do I have? The horses behind us are nosing up. I can feel their breath through my britches. I urge Skee Ball on. I tell him to give it all he's got. Tucker is doing the same with his mount. The four of us—me on Skee Ball and Tucker on Churchill Charlie—move forward as one.

Gimpy glances back and starts in earnest with his whip. He's got a length on us, and he intends to keep it. Tucker and I edge up some more, and we enter the final turn.

All it takes is one slash across Gimpy's thigh with the edge of my whip to buckle his leg. It doesn't cut through his silks, but it'll burn something awful for a couple of days. Heck, I learned that on my first day here.

Gimpy yelps like a dog that stuck its nose in a beehive. He loses his balance, and his chest gets lost in Pratfall's mane.

Pratfall stutters in his step and veers to the outside. It's enough to slow him down.

I swat him again. Right on the same spot.

Gimpy screams out, "You're as good as dead!" He tries to return the blow, but I block his hand with my wrist. He goes for me a second time, but by then Tucker and I are too far ahead.

I hear him calling foul behind me, but his voice gets lost as two other horses overtake him. He might complain to the stewards, but if they didn't see Gimpy grab my boot, they sure as hell didn't see me slash him across the thigh.

Tucker and I stay neck and neck into the homestretch, but Churchill Charlie loses strength in the final sixteenth. Part of me wants to slow down—to let Tucker cross the line first on account of what he did for me. Heck, the guy probably saved my life. But that's only a small part of me.

The rest of me wants to win.

I blow across the finish line so far ahead people probably think I'm trailing the fifth rather than winning the sixth.

I stand up in my irons, tip my cap to Tucker, and head to the winner's circle to celebrate. If coming in the money twice on my debut day in Saratoga didn't already secure my reputation, winning a race where I nearly fell from the saddle—nearly got trampled to death—sure will. If there were stock for jockeys, mine would just have skyrocketed.

20

Oh, by the way," Mr. Hodge says as he saddles up Triple Cherry for the sixth. It's the second Wednesday of the season, and, at three to one, Triple Cherry is favored to do well. She's also one of the prettiest horses in Pelton's stable, a lean and gleaming, roan-colored three-year-old with a shocking red mane. "Your father rang us up," Mr. Hodge goes on. "He's having trouble getting himself here from Albany. No dough and no work."

"You told him I was riding, didn't you?"

"It wasn't me who talked to him." Mr. Hodge tugs the strap and buckles my saddle snug across Triple Cherry's back. "It was Mr. Pelton's girl. She said your father sounded more excited than a schnauzer in a sausage factory on account of what's been going on with you."

"She said that or you said that?"

Mr. Hodge shifts his cigar to the other side and gives me a grin. "All right, I added that last part, about the schnauzer and the sausages, but I reckon he's been devouring those Albany papers. From what I understand, both the *Times Union* and *The Knickerbocker News* cover the goings-on up here at the track pretty well."

"I should go get him."

Mr. Hodge nods. "Probably should. Sounds to me like he's hand to mouth."

Over the past week, I've breezed more than a hundred horses at a buck or two apiece and raced as many ponies as I could get myself on to. On account of my winning that race my very first day and my record ever since, trainers have been after me left and right. I've gotten the reputation of being one of those jockeys who make average horses look good. Mr. Hodge warned me about running myself ragged, but I figure I've got to make money while there's money to make. I take the rides when I can get them.

Sure I haven't been riding all that long, but people follow this stuff. They follow it in the papers. They listen on the radio. It's what they talk about on their way to work and on their way home. They jaw about it over dinner and when they're standing outside church. To top it off, even though it's only got a five-week season, Saratoga is one of the most froufrou tracks in the country. It's always front page of the sports section. Sometimes it's front page of the whole paper. As far as I know, I've never made front page of Sports *or* News—not in any of the rags—but the social pages are another matter entirely.

Short of Manhattan galas and maybe Los Angeles movie premieres, there are few events that see more flashbulbs than the ritzy Saratoga social spots during track season.

After I showed up at the Brook that first night, the gossip reporters have been a little more than interested in me and

Elizabeth. With her pushing six feet without heels and me five and a half on tiptoes, they've been poking fun at our height difference, calling her the Empire State Girlfriend and me King Kong, as if I have to climb up her just to get a kiss. After a little digging, they found out more and have been writing about all sorts of other differences between us too: money, education, family, you name it. At first it made me nervous, but Elizabeth told me to ignore all that hubbub.

One of the writers dubbed me "Shabby" Jack Walsh on account of getting out of the Bugatti in my work clothes, and it stuck. It wasn't the sort of nickname I had hoped for—I wanted something like "Rock Solid" or "The Viper"—but no one picks his own nickname. It just comes to you. It comes to you and sticks with you like polio.

Elizabeth has been taking me to all the nicer places in town—the Union Hotel, the Brook, the Piping Rock, the Adelphi Tea Room. Now, she's trying to convince me to get my own apartment—someplace downtown. I think it's a good idea, but after sleeping in the stalls for the better part of three years, I'm digging my hooves in a little. I think I'd miss being close to the horses, all the nickering and chattering.

A few days earlier, Elizabeth took me on down to a fancy clothing store. It was probably the nicest store I've ever been in. The sleek suit on the mannequin in the front window alone was more expensive than all the clothes I've ever owned. I had to look a second time to make sure it wasn't Al Capone or one of his contemporaries standing there in that window. And I bought myself every last piece of clothing on that mannequin—double-breasted, slate-colored, chalk-stripe suit with padded shoulders and tapered waist, petrol blue tie with white stripes, and matching blue felt hat. I even sprang for new duds for the boys so they'd be able to come out on the town with us.

Bucky's been making time with Elizabeth's friend Jane. They seem like puzzle pieces, the two of them. As for Oatmeal and Pug, they're doing everything they can to keep up with all the girls following us around just because photographers are following us around.

Even after everything I've spent and after I paid back Elizabeth (plus nine dollars interest), I've managed to sock away quite a bankroll. Between breezing and racing and win bonuses, I've got five hundred and fifty-nine bucks. I sit up by lamplight and count it over and over, putting the bills in order of denomination, print date, and then serial number, until I fall asleep. I normally wait until the end of the month to send money home, but I've been giving some thought to sending it sooner. With Jasper lurking around, with every track worker being poorer than poor, it's not so smart to leave all that cash lying around—even if I do keep it tucked so high up in the rafters that only a sparrow could find it.

Mr. Hodge snaps his fingers in front of my nose. "Focus on the work ahead of you," he says. "Get your head out of your ass so you can sit upright in the saddle."

"I'll go to Albany myself and bring my father up here," I tell him. "That is, if I can find him."

Mr. Hodge takes off his hat and picks at some invisible lint. "Do it on a dark day," he says. "I need you here for racing Monday through Saturday. If I were you, I'd check down by the docks. It's where most men in your father's position would go looking for daywork."

"The docks?" I say. "Is that near the train station?"

"Don't rightly know," Mr. Hodge says. He takes my boot

and hoists me up into the saddle. "I understand there are hotels for guys in your father's position—shelters and whatnot—
but if he really doesn't have much money, there're probably
shanties down there too. Hobo jungles. There's no telling.
These are some hard times, Jack. Be much easier if you had a
car . . ."

"THIS ONE IS SMASHING!" Elizabeth says, pointing to the
shiny silver Rolls-Royce sitting in the center of the Crystal
Room at the Union Hotel. "Imagine picking up your father in
that."

"Yeah," I say. "I can just see us rolling around some Albany
shantytown in a Rolls-Royce. We'd be lucky to make it out of
there without someone tossing a brick through the wind-
shield."

As soon as I mentioned needing a car, Elizabeth dragged
me to the Union. It's another of the posh hotels along Broadway and has a reputation for outrageous galas, the best music
on Broadway, and attracting gangsters at the bar. I'm pretty
sure Lucky Luciano himself was down there when we passed
through. The Crystal Room is a long, narrow ballroom lined
on both sides by tall, arched windows. A massive, polished
brass and crystal chandelier hangs from the center of the ceiling and, along with a number of oil streetlamps, illuminates a
dozen or so swanky cars.

"How about this one?" Elizabeth points out a long and low
Duesenberg sitting off to the side. The wheel wells look big
enough to hide a team of Clydesdales. The sign says it's a
Model J LaGrande phaeton. I grab a brochure so I can put it
with the others under my cot. "I think this one should be in
the center of the showroom," she says. "It's a jaw-dropper!"

"I might be inclined to agree with you," a voice says. A man wearing a gray suit and the shiniest shoes I've ever seen comes over and puts out his hand. "Ross Ketchum," he says. "It's a pleasure." He talks fast and it seems each of his words has a period after it, like Mr. Ketchum isn't a car salesman as much as he is a talking Tommy gun.

I shake his hand. "Nice to meet you. I'm—"

"Shabby," he says. "Shabby Jack Walsh. I'd recognize your face anywhere. Heck, there isn't a person in this town who doesn't know who you are. You really came out of the starting gate with a bang."

"He certainly did." Elizabeth sidles up alongside me and grabs my elbow. "He's the finest jockey this side of . . . Well, he's the finest jockey just about anywhere."

Mr. Ketchum smiles. His eyes flick toward the Rolls. "So, I'm guessing you're in the market for an automobile."

"These cars, all of them, are . . . Let's just say I've got Rolls-Royce tastes on a Schwinn bicycle budget."

"I know what you mean. I know what you mean," Mr. Ketchum says, nodding. "I don't even drive one myself, and I sell the darn things. They're more expensive to run than most small countries. And just try to get parts for them."

Mr. Ketchum takes me by the elbow and turns me away from all the fancy cars. "Look here, son. I've got the perfect car for you, but it's not here and it's not in my showroom. What do you say we take a little walk?"

"I don't know," I say, my hand dropping to my pocket. "I've only got—"

"Don't you worry about the money," he says. "I'll cut you a good deal. Just getting my car into those social pages would be better advertising than . . . Heck, you just can't buy that kind of advertising."

I shrug and look at Elizabeth.

She shrugs back. "Let's take a look."

MR. KETCHUM'S GARAGE just south of Congress Park is longer, wider, and higher than any of our barns back home. The amazing thing is that there are no steel support beams. The building is held up by forty-foot timbers so wide a full-grown gorilla couldn't get its arms around one. Rows of cars sit on lifts and are crammed into every other free spot. It's so cluttered I wonder how any work gets done in here. My eyes dart from car to car, all of which are black with the exception of two burgundy sedans and a dark blue coupe. As I eyeball each, I wonder which one Mr. Ketchum has in mind for me. I can't see myself behind the wheel of any of them. Each is stodgier than the last. I know I shouldn't expect too much on a budget like mine, but Mr. Ketchum made it sound like he had something really special—a cherry—waiting for me.

Elizabeth's heels make sharp clacks on the concrete floor. Her nose crinkles up a little more with each car she sees.

"So, what do you think?" Mr. Ketchum says. "See anything you like?"

"Nice cars," I say. The words come out flat, and I hope I don't offend him. I'm sure he understands. After all, this is a guy who sells Rolls-Royces and Duesenbergs at the Union Hotel.

Mr. Ketchum leads me over to one of the delivery trucks and slaps it with an open hand. The bold lettering on the side says: BILL'S MEAT WAGON AND BUTCHERY. "So, what do you think? This one is perfect for you. Just think of the heads you'll turn pulling up to the club in a beauty like this."

"A meat wagon?" Elizabeth says. "You must be joking. They'll wave us around to the service entrance."

A car passes by outside. Its tires rattle down the cobblestone.

"Is there still meat in it?" I ask.

Mr. Ketchum's straight face breaks into a smile. "Come on, Shabby. I'm just twistin' your screw. Follow me." He makes his way around the meat wagon to the rear of the garage—to a smaller car covered with a lily-white tarp.

"Now, I'm going to have to warn you," Mr. Ketchum says, a coltish grin on his face. "This car isn't like anything you've ever seen off a production line. When I made the changes two years ago and put this little baby out in front, I was sure, sure, sure it would bring people to the dealership. I thought it would bring them in droves. Then, Henry Ford himself wrote me a letter."

"Henry Ford? What'd it say?" I ask.

Mr. Ketchum's hand glides along the covered hood of his car as he thinks back. The sharp angles of his face seem to sharpen. "The man pitched a fit. He said he didn't want anything in front of one of his dealerships that a thousand paying customers couldn't come in and buy. So, I brought her inside and covered her up. She hasn't seen the light of day since, except when I tinker with her, of course. I think it might be time for my baby bird to leave the nest."

Mr. Ketchum grabs a fistful of the tarp. "Are you ready?"

Elizabeth and I both nod.

Mr. Ketchum yanks the tarp away. It slides off as if it was made of silk and reveals the nicest piece of machinery I've ever seen. It looks like a 1932 Ford coupe, but different. Very different. It seems to ride lower to the ground than a typical Ford, but the rear of it is somehow jacked up on larger, fatter wheels. The top has been removed and replaced with canvas. And the paint . . . Well, the paint job is spectacular. Most of the car is a glossy light blue, the light blue of a clear morning sky. A jagged silver stripe, like a lightning bolt, runs down the side from the front wheel well to the trunk. I circle the vehicle to the back, where it says: KETCHUM, IF YOU CAN! in fancy silver lettering.

"What do you think?" Mr. Ketchum says proudly.

"What do I think?" I say. "I think it's fantastic!"

"*Fantastic* isn't the word for it," Elizabeth says. "This car is stunning!"

A grin spreads across Mr. Ketchum's face. "You kids ain't seen nothing yet," he says. He unlatches the hood and folds the blue panel up to reveal a motor shinier than the silverware at the Brook. It's got to be the shiniest motor anyone's ever seen. "I had each piece shipped to a special plant downstate, where they chromed it, polished it, and sent it back up," he says. "The guys down there thought I had lost a few lug nuts paying what I paid to have it done. Isn't she a beauty?"

"It's a work of art," Elizabeth says.

"Yeah, well, the good folks at the old Ford Motor Company didn't think so." Mr. Ketchum leans over the engine. "Not to mention I've made a few of my own modifications. She ain't just pretty. She's got teeth!"

Mr. Ketchum slides into the front seat and starts her up. The car growls to life, and I can't help but stare at that gleaming V-8, the four exhaust pipes on each side sloping down, merging into one, pushing out the sweet smell of car exhaust.

"I wonder," I say to Mr. Ketchum. "Could we run this machine with the hood off? You know, the way men do it in the Grand Prix races? It'd be a shame to drive her down the road and hide what she's got going on inside."

Mr. Ketchum chews on my idea for a second and nods. "That's a right good idea," he says. "Let's make it happen."

Within seconds, Mr. Ketchum has the hood off. He wraps the panels in cheesecloth and carefully leans them against the wall.

Elizabeth steps around the car and gets into the passenger seat. "How much?" she asks him.

"Lizzy," I say. "Let me handle this. I'll speak with Mr. Ketchum and—"

"How much?" she says to Mr. Ketchum again, this time more firmly.

"Right to the point, huh?" Mr. Ketchum scratches his cleanly shaven face. "I haven't given it much thought," he says. He slides in next to Elizabeth and revs the engine a few times. "After all, between the paint, the chrome, the superchargers, and the other extra parts, I've sunk at least a thousand into her. She's my baby."

"Come on now," Elizabeth says. "You said it before. You can't *buy* publicity like this. Consider it part of your advertising budget. This car is going to be in all the papers."

"Wait a second," I say. "I'm just starting out here. I'm not sure—"

Elizabeth shoots me a glance, and I shut my mouth. "We'll give you five hundred for it," she says.

"Five hundred? Five hundred is less than the car's worth without modifications."

"Who's going to buy a car like this aside from us?" Eliza-

beth says. "Five hundred and we'll let you leave your little ad-
vertisement on the back. Everyone will see it."

"Eight hundred," he says.

I don't have eight hundred dollars, and even if I did I
wouldn't spend it on a car. I move to step in, but Elizabeth's
glare stops me again. "Six hundred," she says. "Think about it,
Mr. Ketchum. This is going to be like a spark in a fireworks
factory for your business. Anyhow, this car of yours is a
'thirty-two. It's two years old already. What are you going to
do? Sell it as used?"

"Seven, then," he says. "Seven hundred dollars. But I want a
few good tips from Shabby here before the season is through."

Elizabeth leans across the seat and shakes Mr. Ketchum's
hand. "You've got yourself a deal. Seven hundred dollars and a
few tips." She turns to me. "Jack, pay the man."

I start patting at my pockets as though I've left my real
billfold, the big one with all the money, in my other set of
trousers. "I'm not sure I'm carrying that much on me," I say.

"How about you stop by Friday?" Mr. Ketchum suggests.
"I'd like a few days to get her ready for you anyhow."

Elizabeth nods. "Very good, then. It's nice doing business
with you, Mr. Ketchum."

"Call me Ross," he says to her.

"Ross it is."

As we make our way across the street, I start harping on
Elizabeth. "Seven hundred dollars?" I say. "I haven't got seven
hundred dollars! The most I can put together is five and
change. And the bulk of that is headed home to my family."

Elizabeth stops in the middle of the street and turns to me.
"First of all, hang on to your money. You're going to need it
more than your family does. Haven't you ever heard that

you've got to spend money to make money? Second, I'll give you another loan if you need to bridge the gap. I've got cash."

"That's not the point!" I say. "I shouldn't be buying a seven-hundred-dollar car in the first place. I shouldn't be buying *any* car! Seven hundred dollars is more than my father makes in a whole year. I should hire a cab to take me down to Albany to find my dad. But instead, you just bulldozed your way into me buying a car I have no business buying."

"It's too late now. You shook on it."

"No," I say. "*You* shook on it."

Elizabeth strips off her long gloves and stuffs them in her purse. "There are plenty of reasons why you need that car, Jack."

"Name them."

"All right." She starts ticking the reasons off on her perfectly enameled fingers. "First, you need to erupt on the social scene around here. I know you don't understand it, but I do. I've grown up around this. When people know who you are, for either good reasons or bad, you matter more. In the world of horse racing, mattering more means getting better rides. That means more money. Owners want famous riders because they bring more attention to their horses. When owners think of riders, I want them to think Shabby Jack Walsh. I want people to open the paper and search for Shabby Jack Walsh. Consider this car an investment."

"But—"

She goes on, plowing right over my words. "Showboat knew it," she says. "Showboat was as flashy as they come, and everybody knew his name. He was riding the best horses in the country, Jack, and it's not because he was the best jockey. Just look at his stats."

Mr. Hodge's advice rings in my head. Is this what he meant? Does this have something to with Be-Do-Achieve? I remind myself to think on it when I don't have Elizabeth staring me down with those big hazel eyes of hers.

"Second," Elizabeth goes on. "That car you just bought is beautiful—no, not beautiful, that car is dazzling. I don't know where Mr. Ketchum came up with his design, but it is inspired. I'd go so far as to say that car is nicer than my father's Bugatti!"

"Well, I don't know about that—"

"It's one of a kind, Jack. No one else in the world drives a car like that. If a car can be considered a work of art, that one is the *Venus de Milo!*"

"I'm sure there's a third reason . . . ," I say.

"Of course there's a third reason." Elizabeth smiles, and that little wrinkle in her forehead melts me like ice in hot soup. "I want you to have that car. I want *us* to have that car. I want to show up at the Brook in it—with the top down and that engine growling—and I want to see so many flashbulbs pop that I'm seeing stars for weeks."

Then, she kisses me, and it's not one of her usual kisses— the ones she's been dishing out for the past week—where she turns her head just so and opens her lips barely enough for me to get a hint of what's past them. No, this kiss is a full-on, open-mouth, legendary kind of kiss that makes me realize no matter what she says, no matter what she asks me to do, I'll still come back for more.

"I'm sold," I say. "Let's buy that car."

She smiles a lipstick-smudged smile. "I knew you'd see it my way."

21

"P ARDON MY FRENCH," PUG SCREAMS FROM THE BACK-
seat, "but *ay, carajo!*"

"That's Spanish, stupid," Oatmeal says. I know the punch
is coming before I hear Pug cry out in pain.

"Where'd you get this beauty?" Bucky asks. He pokes his
head between Elizabeth and me. "You make a deal with the
devil or something?"

I smile at Elizabeth, who, as usual, has her feet up on the
dashboard. I think of the money I owe her. As quickly as I
dug myself out of debt with her, I found myself right back in.
"I'm not sure," I say. "Maybe I did."

The past few days brought a lot of morning workouts and
more freelance rides than I expected. And I'll have to admit, I
rode pretty well, which got me some fresh dough. The three-
year-old allowance race I won this afternoon alone earned me
a clean hundred, but I sent a few C-notes home to my family
in the hopes that whatever trouble my father found himself
in, whatever trouble brought him out to Albany looking for

work, will go away. It's true that money comes fast when you're a winning jockey, but the whole ugly truth is that it disappears even quicker.

As we make our way down Broadway, I tap my foot on the gas pedal. The engine growls, and the car surges forward in small bursts. Elizabeth laughs as I shake her up. She's drinking in all the attention—all the heads turning, all the fingers pointing, and all the talking and guessing about who might be driving such a strange-looking automobile.

Mr. Ketchum did a great job getting the car ready for us. The paint job is even shinier than when we saw it in the garage, and he must have polished the engine part by part. He even painted the words NOT TOO SHABBY! in silver along the door in honor of my new nickname.

"We'll stop by Jane's house and pick her up," Elizabeth says. "Her family rents a place on Division Street."

"There ain't no room back here for Jane," Oatmeal says.

"Oh, I'll find room," Bucky says.

"After we get her, we'll head over to the Brook," Elizabeth says.

"The Brook!" Pug screams out. "I love the Brook!"

"You love the Brook?" I say. "You lost twenty bucks of mine in one spin of the roulette wheel last time we were there."

"Right, and I need to get it back for you," Pug says. "I just need to borrow five dollars first."

ELIZABETH WAS SPOT-ON when she said we'd cause a stir the first time we pulled up to the Brook. People stare at us as though the circus has come to town. Even though the driveway is packed with the likes of the Whitneys and the Rockefellers and the Fitzsimmonses, the reporters swarm around our car and take photo after photo of Shabby Jack Walsh and his chums.

I'll have to admit I sort of like the attention. I mean, two weeks ago most of these people wouldn't have stopped to let me shine their shoes. Now that I'm riding at Saratoga Race Course, everyone wants to talk to me. Everyone wants to buy me a drink. Heck, everyone wants to know what shaving powder I use. Most of the reporters and photographers have to stay behind a velvet rope and call out questions from the crowd, but the ones from the real big rags get to stand wherever they like. Publicity like this sells a lot of steaks, and the Brook is all about selling steaks. Steaks, booze, and rolls of the dice.

"Oh!" Jane giggles. She stands on the backseat and waves to the reporters like she already is a movie star. "Hello to all my adoring fans!"

The questions come at us like pecks from a typewriter:

"Where'd you get the car?"

"Shabby, any news about an engagement?"

"How'd you turn that lazy filly into a contender in the third today?"

"Any thoughts of going out West to one of the new tracks?"

"Seriously, Shabby, where'd you get the car?"

I step out and walk around to help Elizabeth. The boys, dressed up in their new duds, hop out of the open top, their shiny shoes landing heavy on the driveway. Bucky helps Jane, and I can't help but smile at the looks on all those stuffy fat cats' faces. I grab Elizabeth's wrist and turn to dash inside, but she clutches my hand, pulls me to her side, and spins to face the reporters.

"The car is from Mr. Ross Ketchum at Ketchum Motors,"

Elizabeth calls out to them. "That filly from the third is my father's, and it would do you well not to call her lazy. As for going out West, Shabby has no plans to do so. After all, I'm a New York City girl." She wiggles her left hand to the crowd. "And as you can see, we're not engaged, but I can assure you boys that you'll be the first to know!"

She blows the reporters a kiss, and we rush inside the club. Within moments, the manager brings us to our table like we're some kind of royalty. It's one of those high-backed booths along the rear of the dining room. From where we're sitting, we can see the entertainment on the stage and hear the roars of excitement from the gaming room.

"Hey, Jack," Bucky says after we get our first round of drinks. "We need you to settle another bet for us."

"Whatcha got this time?"

"We were wondering who's got the longest streak of wins."

"The longest streak of wins?" I say.

"You know," Pug says. "Who won the most races in a row."

"I know what a streak is," I say.

"I keep telling them it's got to be Albert Adams," Bucky says. "He won nine consecutive in September of 1930."

"There's one better," I say. "Last year, Gordon Richards rode twelve straight winners."

"Twelve straight?" Pug says. "No one's ridden twelve straight winners. And if someone did, we'd have heard of him."

"He did it in England," I say.

"England?" Oatmeal says. "England doesn't count!"

"They've been racing in England a lot longer than they've been doing it here," Pug says, pointing to Oatmeal with his glass.

"That's true," Bucky adds. "And the three original Thoroughbreds were from England."

"Oh, I love it! You boys are so deep!" Jane cries out like she just saw a drowsy kitten fall into its milk. She grabs Bucky's face and kisses him full on the lips in front of everyone. "If anyone wants this boy," she says, "they're going to have to go through me to get him."

Bucky looks stunned. Happy as all hell, but stunned.

"You can keep him," Pug says. "He snores."

Bucky grabs a roll and tosses it at Pug. It bounces off his forehead and onto his plate.

"So, what do you think?" Oatmeal says to me. "Who's got the longest streak? Should we go with America only, or do you think England should count?"

"What about the horses?" Elizabeth asks.

"What about them?" Pug says.

"There are horses with better winning streaks than the jockeys." Elizabeth takes a sip of champagne. "Hindoo had eighteen stakes wins in a row. Then there are losing streaks. Steve Donoghue rode a hundred and eight consecutive losers."

"This is getting complicated," Pug says.

"There are some other great records in racing too," I say. "Levi Barlinume rode until last year, when he fell from his horse and broke his leg."

"What's so special about that?" Bucky says.

"He was eighty years old."

"What about the lightest jockey?" Elizabeth says. I feel her foot glide across my shin under the table. A tingle creeps up my leg.

"Who's the lightest?" Oatmeal says.

"Another Englishman," she says. "Kitchner was his name. He weighed forty-nine pounds when he rode Red Deer to win the 1844 Chester Cup."

"Forty-nine pounds?" I say, thinking of the three pounds I need to lose for post time tomorrow.

Elizabeth holds up a gloved finger. "They say he weighed forty a few years earlier."

"That guy must have been around three years old!" Pug says.

Bucky clinks his glass with his fork. "I think we can agree that no one owes no one a quarter this time," he says. "But Oatmeal still owes me two, and Pug still owes me four."

"Jack," Pug says, sinking into his seat. "Pay the guy four quarters for me."

"And give him two for me while you're at it," Oatmeal adds.

"If you'll excuse us," Elizabeth says, touching my shoulder. "Jane and I have to go powder our noses. She's got some lipstick work to do."

I slide out of the booth and let Elizabeth and Jane out. We all stand, and I hand Elizabeth her purse. After they've gone, we all sit back down.

"So what do you think?" Bucky says, leaning over the table toward us. "Is she the most gorgeous little filly in the world, or what?"

"I'm not so sure," Oatmeal says. "I'll let you know when I've had a chance to breeze her."

Bucky smacks Oatmeal in the shoulder. "You'd better not go near her," he says. "I have a feeling about this one."

"What kind of feeling?" I say.

Bucky reaches across the table and grabs a roll. He stuffs it in his mouth. "You know . . . that feeling."

"She's the only girl you've ever said more than three words to," Pug says. "How can you be so sure?"

"Not to mention you've only known her for about a week," Oatmeal adds.

"Guys," Bucky says, sitting back in his chair, "a man knows when a man knows."

Pug takes a huge bite of his roll. "Well, let me know when the *man* gets here," he says.

As soon as the girls get back from whatever girls do when they powder their noses, we order and eat. Elizabeth, as usual, gets the beef Wellington, and Jane gets the rack of lamb. The boys and I all get steaks. Mine's a fillet, and each bite practically melts in my mouth. Before I know it, my plate is clean—vegetables and all. My belly feels just about ready to burst.

I pull my napkin from my lap and rest it on the edge of the table. "If you'll excuse me . . . ," I say.

"You look a little green," Bucky says to me. "You need a hand? After all, I am your valet."

"I'll be fine. I just need a minute."

I make my way to the bathroom and head straight for the stall. If I'd gotten there a second later, I'd have made an awful mess, but all the contents of my stomach manage to make it into the bowl. I heave and heave until I feel like there's nothing left to get out. Then, I heave some more, until only stringy goo drips down. I cough, and my throat burns like I've just gargled with lye. The purging is getting easier, though.

As I kneel there to see if I can get any more out, I hear the bathroom door open. Someone whispers. The attendant mumbles something back. Another wave of heaves grabs hold of me, and I can't see or hear anything on account of all the pressure in my head and the ringing in my ears.

When I open my eyes, it's dark. A *whomp, whomp, whomp-ing* comes up behind me. Before I can spin around, the door to the stall bursts open and knocks me forward. Someone grabs me by the hair. Strong hands. Brutal hands. They shove me down until my head plunges into the water. Vomit water. I hold my breath until my chest feels about to explode. My arms flail, but I can feel only the toilet paper roll and two tree-trunk legs. Shoes. I feel shoes and trousers. I try to jerk my head out of the water, but I can't. My fingers scramble for a hold, and I grab an ankle. An ankle with no sock.

The hands pull me out of the toilet and practically lift me off the ground. "You're going to sponge that horse," Jasper says. "You're going to sponge that horse and that's the last I'm gonna tell you."

I cough and sputter and gasp for breath.

I feel him stuff a sponge into my jacket pocket.

"You're gonna sponge that horse or that pretty little girl-friend of yours . . . let's just say that she'll be going on a date with me and a few of my buddies."

"No!"

"Now, I'm a perfect gentleman around the ladies," Jasper hisses, "especially with a girl that sweet and innocent, but I can't speak too highly for my friends. Their tastes . . . Well, their tastes are a little rough around the edges, if you catch my meaning."

I realize I'm nodding.

Jasper's grip tightens, and he shakes me like a dusty horse blanket. "The Bolton Stakes is coming up, and I don't have a serious commitment from you. I've got no assurances. So, I want you to say it," he says. "I want you to tell me you're going to sponge that horse."

"I'll do it," I sputter through my tears. "I'll sponge Fire-side."

"See that you do."

Jasper drops me, and I squeeze my eyes shut. I listen to him leave the bathroom, trying my best to hold back my sobs. They come anyway. I lock the stall and sink to the floor.

22

DO YOU SERIOUSLY BELIEVE WE'RE GOING TO FIND him down here?" Elizabeth says as we roll through the maze of boarded-up buildings that is the Port of Albany. "These shantytowns go on forever."

"We have to find him," I say. "Now that I see how bad it is down here, well, it's just tearing me up. I mean, we were eating steaks and dancing last night. All the while these people are close to starving."

Elizabeth folds her hands in her lap and slides away from the car door, closer to me. "Well, I'm just not comfortable."

I leave the Ford in first gear and let it purr up and down the narrow roads near the Hudson River. Scrap-wood shacks with sheet-metal roofs line the streets. Men and women sit idly on boxes and overturned cans. Children, faces smeared with grime, sit in rows along the curbs. I thought it was tough living in a horse stall, but seeing people living like this makes me realize that I don't have it all that bad. Heads turn, eyes stare, as my baby blue beauty weaves through the streets. I knew from the beginning that I shouldn't have bought this car. I argued with Elizabeth about it. I knew it wasn't right. That money would've been better spent on bread for all these struggling people. Instead, I spent seven hundred dollars on a one-of-a-kind car because of a kiss from a girl.

A legendary kiss, sure, but a kiss nonetheless.

I scan the hundreds, no, thousands of people for that familiar face. The square jaw. The salt-and-pepper hair. The crooked teeth. But it's hopeless. Half the people are huddled in circles, their backs to the street. If I had a dozen dark days—a dozen days to search Albany—and everyone was standing shoulder to shoulder on the edge of the road, I doubt I'd come close to finding my father.

We started off asking around at the docks, but no one knew him. After we threw enough money around, one guy said he'd met someone who fit my father's description, including the fact that he'd come from someplace near Syracuse. He sent us over here. I hope we'll find him soon. I don't like the looks I'm getting from some of these folks.

"This is hopeless," Elizabeth says. "There're thousands of people. We don't know if your father is working or not. We're not even sure if he's still in Albany. He might've made his way to Troy or one of the other textile towns. These people, they roam around like hoboes."

I pound my fist on the steering wheel. *"Hoboes?"* I say. "Just because my father is struggling, just because he's doing what he needs to do to support his family, just because he's down on his luck, that doesn't make him a hobo!"

"Just settle down, baby." Elizabeth tries to take my hand, but I pull away.

"Don't tell me to settle down. This is my father you're talk-

ing about. I haven't seen him for over three years, and now
the man doesn't have enough money to take a one-hour train
ride to Saratoga. He's penniless and hungry, and he's probably
wandering the streets someplace."

"Look, I'm sorry, Jack. I didn't mean it that way. It's just
that we've been doing this for hours, and this place . . . well,
like I said, it makes me uncomfortable. I know how important this is to you—and if it's important to you, it's important
to me. But this place . . . I never knew people lived like this."

I've seen poor people. There were poor people who trav-
eled from farm to farm during apple harvest. There were poor
people when I was running the circuit with Tweed. Heck, up
until a few weeks ago I was a poor person—me and all the
boys. What shocks me here is just how many of them there
are in one place. Albany is a sea of poverty, and I'm too
ashamed to admit that I'm as surprised as she is.

Elizabeth strokes my hand, and this time I let her. "Let's
find your father, then," she says.

We wind through the shantytown for a while longer, until I
decide to get on over to the South End before the sun goes
down. Someone told me earlier there were a few more settle-
ments down there. We make our way along the riverfront,
through the port, where every factory seems closed down,
gates shut. A sign hangs on each one that says, NO MEN
WANTED.

"You know," I say, "I was thinking on something."

"What's that?"

I know this isn't going to go over well, but after last night
at the Brook—after what Jasper said he'd do to Elizabeth—I
have to do something. I wouldn't mind so much him pounding me into gravy, but if he lays a hand on Elizabeth, I'd never

forgive myself. "I was thinking . . . ," I say. "I was thinking it might be a good idea if you went home to New York City for a week or so."

"That's ridiculous. You know I have a business to run."

"Seriously," I say. "I think it's a good idea."

Elizabeth's stare nearly burns the side of my face. "Jack? What are you saying?"

"I was just thinking—"

"Yes, I heard you the first time." She leans toward me. She rests her chin on my shoulder so she's practically whispering in my ear. "What's the matter? Don't you fancy me anymore? Don't you like the feeling of my lips on yours?"

I downshift the car, and it bucks a little as it slows. "Of course I like all that stuff, Lizzy. Heck, I'm crazy about you. Things are just getting a little complicated right now."

"Whatever's troubling you, it's nothing we can't handle together." Elizabeth puts her hand over mine. "Think of it like all those mediocre horses you turn into winners. Sure, it might look grim when you get up in the saddle, when you think about how that horse didn't come in the money in its last six outings, but once you've got the reins in your hands and you get yourself loaded into that gate, all kinds of ideas and opportunities present themselves. That's what you're good at, Jack. And this time I can help you."

I return her hand to her lap and shift gears. "This isn't a horse race, Elizabeth. This is something serious. Something more important."

"There's nothing more important than a horse race," she says.

"There is to me."

I glance over at her and see her huge hazel eyes staring at me. They look worried. I've never seen such worried-looking eyes, and I decide to tell her everything.

"There's a guy threatening me."

"Threatening you?"

I nod. "And now he's threatening you."

"Why would someone threaten me?"

"It has something to do with fixing a race—tampering with one of our horses," I say. "I don't want to do it. I turned the money down and told the guy to shove off, but . . . let's just say that the guy hasn't been so easy to shake."

"What does he want you to do?" she asks.

It's a whole lot easier to tell Elizabeth about this than it was to tell Bucky. At least she doesn't work in the same stable. At least she's not shooting for the same job as I am. At least she's not broke and likely to let slip exactly what she's not supposed to let slip. "They want me to sponge Fireside," I say.

Elizabeth lets my words sink in like they're sitting in the oven and she's trying to let them bake all the way through.

"Sponging means—"

"I know what sponging means," she says. "Fireside? Why him?"

"He's running in the Bolton Stakes next week. It's a twenty-thousand-dollar purse, winner takes all. I'm supposed to ride Fireside, and this guy doesn't want him in the picture. At first, when I was just an exercise boy, the guy offered me two hundred dollars to do it. Ever since I told him to take a hike, the guy has been straight out threatening me. The money's off the table, and now he's threatening to do something to you. Something bad."

"Fireside, though?"

"He's a great horse. He has a lot of potential. And he's got a real chance to win."

"What makes you so sure?"

"Up until two weeks ago, I rode him almost every day," I say. "I've seen that horse grow, improve. Heck, I've felt it. How he eats up that track. How he pushes himself no matter what. I know he's got it in him. He's the best horse I've ever ridden. And with me in the saddle, we can blow the field away. It seems this guy—and whoever's paying him—feels the same way."

"Who's the guy asking you to do it?"

"His name is Jasper Cunningham."

Elizabeth shrugs. "I've never heard of him."

"You sure? You've grown up around the track."

"Why would I lie about something like that?" she says. "What does he look like?"

"He's big, he's tough, and he doesn't wear socks. He talks with his mouth full, and it doesn't look like 'no' is on the list of words he understands."

Elizabeth seems to chew on what I've told her. As we cross the railway tracks, she turns to me. "Do it," she says.

"Do it?"

She nods. "Just do it. Throw the race. Jockeys do it all the time."

"I don't know . . ."

"What's not to know?" she says. "It's a contract ride. If you win, you get a ten-dollar bonus from Mr. Pelton. Ten bucks. You can make that in a half morning of breeze work now. Why put yourself in danger, Jack? Why put me in danger? Throw the race."

What she's suggesting makes sense, but throwing a race . . . It's against everything I've ever learned. Mr. Pelton is counting on Fireside. Mr. Hodge is counting on me. Not to mention, the way Jasper thinks he can just push me around sends acid pulsing through my veins.

"It just don't sit right with me," I say. I turn at the next corner and drop the car back into first. More rows of scrap-wood shacks line the streets.

"It seems to me you're asking for trouble if you don't do what this Jasper guy wants. Not to mention the fact that you're putting me at risk. Is that what you want? Do you want me to get hurt?"

"No," I say.

"Then throw the race."

"I can't—"

"Of course you can," she says, squeezing my thigh. "Heck, if it's a money issue, Jack, I'll beef up the odds on Fireside. It'll draw my girls into betting him. I'll split every dollar I make on Fireside—on that whole race—with you."

My hands tighten on the steering wheel.

"So, it's settled," she says. "You throw the race, this Jasper fellow goes away, we all make money, and I get to stay with you. Everyone's happy." She leans over and kisses my ear. "I told you we could solve this problem together." Then, she snuggles up next to me. "It's starting to get cold. I should have brought my wrap." Her hand slides up on my thigh, and it takes everything I've got to keep my mind on the road.

We snake through the shantytowns and hobo jungles for a while longer, until it gets too dark to see anything—until I realize that all the driving in the world isn't going to bring me any closer to finding my father. I worry that the next time I'll have to get down here is next Sunday, a week away. I'll tell Mr. Pelton's girl to find out where my father is staying if he happens to call again. Maybe I can sneak down here after the races one night and get him. I steer the car onto Route 9 and head north, back to Saratoga.

IN THE END, after all my looking, it's my father who finds me. As soon as Elizabeth and I arrive in town, we head on over to the Jockey Y to meet the boys. The Y is a low building that sits across the street from the main track, on the grounds of the Oklahoma Training Track. It's nothing more than a big, open room with dark-paneled walls and a few lazy ceiling fans. There are a bunch of billiard tables, some card tables, and plenty of pieces of big leather furniture to lounge around on. It's open only to track workers, so at eleven o'clock the place is all but deserted. Any track worker with a brain is long asleep by now.

The boys are most of the way through a bottle of something labeled AÑEJO and are wrestling with lighting cigars bigger than the ones I've seen Mr. Pelton smoke. Pug, his cigar dangling from his fingers, looks like he's past green and into a grayish paisley.

While Elizabeth entertains Oatmeal at the billiard table and Pug sits on a sofa to stare at the tile floor, I pull Bucky aside. We sit in worn leather armchairs across a small coffee table from each other and I tell him how I let Elizabeth in on the whole Jasper situation. He almost goes apoplectic until I tell him how she agreed I should throw the race.

"I knew I liked her," Bucky says. "Gal's got more than cotton batting between her ears."

"Are you saying I've got cotton batting between *my* ears?"

"I didn't say that."

"Actually, you sort of did."

"Why do you always got to assume everything's about you?" Bucky puffs on his cigar a few times. "And why do people smoke these things in the first place? They taste like dried-up horse muck."

Hinges squeak behind me, and I whirl around. The front door of the Jockey Y swings open, and someone steps in. "So, is this what Shabby Jack Walsh does with his free time? Smoking stogies? Drinking booze?"

I recognize the deep voice immediately, and my heart starts fluttering like an excited bird. He steps out of the shadows, and I see that I'm on the money. It's my father. He's aged more than I expected, as though his past few years have been even harder than mine. Deep lines score his face, and what hair he's got left is streaked with gray. I leap from my seat and dive into his arms. He hugs me tight, and I can smell sweat and grease in the fabric of his shirt. It's the smell of hard work. I hug him tighter, and he rocks me back and forth until I let go. When I do, Elizabeth is at my side.

"Elizabeth Reed," she says, shaking his hand. "You must be Mr. Walsh. I've heard so much about you."

"You have?"

"Jack just won't stop talking about you, sir."

My father smiles. "Pleasure to meet you, young lady," he says. "I gather that my son and you are friends?"

"That's right, Mr. Walsh."

"Well, it's good to know that he's been in such good hands in the absence of his mom and pop."

"It's a pleasure to meet you as well," Elizabeth says, "but I'm sure you and Jack have a lot to talk about . . ." She does a slight curtsy—a curtsy!—and starts herding the boys toward the door. "Let's get going," she says to them, and before her voice stops echoing off the walls, the whole lot of them are gone.

My father and I stare at each other for the longest time. I have no idea where to begin—what to tell him first—and I'm guessing he doesn't either.

"I—I looked all over the place for you," I say. "Elizabeth and me, we were down in Albany all day. I couldn't find you anywhere."

My father lays a hand on my shoulder. "There've been no jobs for days down at the port. No job means no money. No money means no train ticket. It was looking hopeless. Then, the strangest thing happened. It was like seeing an angel descend from on high."

"What was?" I say.

"I had my things packed and I was making my way toward the rail yard. I was thinking that maybe I should head back home. Your mother's been on her own for a while now. I was going to hop on the next boxcar headed west when an old-model Ford truck came rambling around the corner. It pulled alongside me, and you'll never guess who got out."

I know Mr. Hodge has an old-model Ford truck. It would be nice to think that he was the one who went down to the port to find my father. The problem is that Mr. Hodge has no idea what my father looks like. In all my years since leaving the farm, I've known only one other person who has an old-model Ford truck.

The door to the Jockey Y swings open. It slams against the outside of the building. A man walks in, almost filling the doorway as he enters. Even when he gets inside, he stands there with his fists on his hips as though this whole room, this place that usually has more than enough space for dozens of people, isn't large enough to hold him.

Tweed McGowan takes off his straw hat. He smiles the smile that took me only a night to learn to hate and says, "Hey there, Jack, m'boy."

23

RAIN HAMMERS DOWN ON THE TIN ROOF OF THE BARN. It's too muggy to get underneath the blankets, so I lie on top in my undershorts. My father sits on the apple crate next to my cot. He rubs my shoulder. I try my best not to tense up, but it happens anyway.

His voice is exactly as I remember it, only a little deeper and a little scratchier. "What's that?" He points to the betting slip with the words "Be-Do-Achieve" written on it that I tacked to the wall.

I figure he wouldn't understand, and I worry that he'll think it's ridiculous, so I don't fill him in. "Just something stupid."

"Busy schedule tomorrow?"

"I'm riding in the first, second, fourth, sixth, and eighth. All but two are freelance. The sixth is looking good. I'll probably make some money there."

"The sixth, huh?"

I almost tell him not to bet on what I think—that I'm

wrong more than I'm right—but then I remember he hasn't got any money to wager. "Happy Go Lucky is a great colt," I say.

I stay up most of the night with my father. He tells me about how the bank foreclosed on the farm because of back taxes and how the family had to move to a small apartment in Syracuse. Fortunately, the postmaster in our little village has been friends with my father since they were in school together. He's been forwarding my envelopes along to them. My pop tells me how my grandfather died in his sleep in that Syracuse apartment and how they weren't able to bury him out on the hill next to my grandmother. He tells me about Penny and how big she's gotten and how she looks forward to my letters every month. When he tells me she's reading and writing some, it makes me realize how long I've been away. Maybe I'll take a drive out there and see her before I head back down to Belmont.

"Look, Son, I'm proud of you—everything you're doing here, the name you're making for yourself. You really took that teach-a-man-to-fish thing to heart."

My mind goes back to the day he sent me off with Tweed.

"Thanks," I say.

My father leans against the wall and slides his palms down the fronts of his trousers. "You know, though, I think it's time we reined in some of this spending."

We? Did he just say "we"?

I look at him looking at me. He doesn't blink.

"Have I ever missed sending money home—even once?" I say.

"It just seems like you're spending a small fortune these days," he says. "Between that car outside and those spiffy new clothes and what you're probably lending your chums . . . Do you think those guys will ever pay you back? You've got to learn to hang on to your money, Jack. People are starving out there."

"Elizabeth knows a lot about this stuff," I say. "According to her—"

"Elizabeth seems like a sweet gal, but how can you be so sure she's got your best interests in mind? Or your family's? What you need to do is start saving."

I know he's right. I *have* been pretty free with my cash. But this whole world is new to me. After all the crap I've had to put up with, I figure I deserve a few weeks of the high life. And who's my father to talk to me about being wise with money? Did he ever save a red cent? If he had, maybe my mother and the rest of them wouldn't be living in some flea trap in Syracuse. Maybe my grandfather could've been buried on the farm next to Grandma like he wanted and not cut up by a bunch of shaky-handed medical students or whatever it is they do with folks who can't afford a proper burial.

"Jack, look at me."

I don't. I stare at the silver shadows that play across the ceiling. Each flicker of lightning makes the rafters come alive.

"If you get hurt or if your fortunes turn upside down, do you think Elizabeth is going to stick around? Do you think she's with you no matter what?"

"I don't know," I say.

"Well, that's something you've got to figure out. It's impor-tant."

The last thing I need is my father lecturing me on girls. Hell, I don't need him lecturing me on anything. I've been on

my own for three years now. I can figure things out by myself.
"I'll get right on it," I say.

"You do that." My father folds his jacket over his arm and
shifts in his seat. "By the way, I was thinking . . ."

"Yeah?"

"Maybe there's something your old man could do around
here. You know, something on the inside—something around
the track."

"Dad, Thoroughbreds aren't anything like the draft horses
back home."

"I know. I know. I was just thinking maybe there was
something, anything." He combs his fingers through his hair.
"It sure would beat trying to rustle up daywork at the facto-
ries every morning."

"If you think of something you want to do around here, let
me know," I say. "I'll see what I can do."

"Now that you mention it, I was wondering if it would be
all right if Tweed and me worked together on your behalf . . .
you know, as your agent. Tweed and I go way back—back to
the days when he was trading horses to pull farm plows and
carts. He did a lot of business with your grandfather, and we
owe a lot to that man. Tweed and I, we'd both get you mounts
and we'd split the profits. The two of us discussed the idea on
the drive up here to Saratoga. Tweed said he'd already talked
about agent work with you some, but you never gave him a
clear answer."

"Whose idea was it—this agenting stuff—yours or his?"

"What's that got to do with anything?"

"Whose idea was it?" I say again.

My father hesitates. "It was Tweed's idea."

I think back to that night at the Brook—the night Pietro threw Tweed out on his keister. My answer couldn't have been clearer. I said in no uncertain terms that Tweed should take a hike, but looking at my father sitting there like a hungry puppy staring at a steak, I can't help myself. My father doesn't know his way around the track. He can't do it alone.

"Let me think on it," I say.

He sits up a little taller. "Maybe the three of us could have dinner tomorrow to get it all figured out?"

"I've got plans with Elizabeth tomorrow. You work it out with Tweed and let me know what you come up with."

"That's a good boy." He shifts forward on his crate and lets out a deep breath. "That's a real good boy. It's tough out there. I don't think you know quite how tough it is."

"I know all about it."

My father's hand finds its way to my shoulder again. "You've done your father proud by what you're doing. You know that, right?"

I'm not used to getting compliments, so I don't say anything back.

Then, he hits me with a doozy.

"Jack, you have a brother."

"I have a what?" I jerk my shoulder away.

"His name is Malachi. He's two and a half now—be three in October."

A crack of thunder shakes the barn. Fireside whinnies on the other side of the wall. I hear him shuffle around and blow out his nostrils. The rain drums harder on the roof, and I have to raise my voice to be heard over it.

"Malachi? What kind of name is that?"

"Your mother says it's biblical. I've wanted to tell you, but money's so tight and you move around so much . . ."

I sit up in my cot and swing my feet to the floor. The dirt is cold, moist. My father goes on about how Penny loves to dress Malachi up and have tea parties with him, but the words drop away. I can hear only a buzzing in my head.

Two and a half years old.

Two and a half years old.

Two and a half years old.

I think back and realize how my mother must have been pregnant when I went off with Tweed. She got pregnant when she was already thinning out the soup—when they couldn't afford to feed the ones they already had. Just like when Tweed sent me off with Mr. Hodge, I guess it was good riddance to bad garbage. Out with the old and in with the new.

I clench my blankets in my fist. "I need to get some shut-eye," I say. "I've got to be up early. I have a ton of breeze work in the morning."

"I knew this'd be hard on you, Son. This is exactly why I didn't want to tell you by telephone."

"I can't talk about this right now—"

"Jack, I—"

"No!" I squeeze the blankets harder until my hands shake like two rattlesnake tails. "It's been more than two years," I say. "It's been more than two years and you haven't found a way to tell me that I have a brother?"

"I've wanted to let you know so many times, but the longer I waited the harder it was. It was just—"

"There's a stall at the end of the shed row," I say. "Take one of the blankets if you want, but I need to get some sleep. I have a job."

"Jack, that ain't fair."

"It's fair as all get out," I say. "I've spent the last three years of my life doing hard labor because you couldn't afford to keep me around. You couldn't afford to keep me around because you were too busy making babies without thinking about how you'd feed them. Now things start looking up for me, and you show up on my doorstep telling me how to spend my money and asking me for a job. You talk about how hard things have been for you and the family, but you haven't given a minute's thought to how hard things have been on me."

My father stands and puts his hand on the stall door. "Jack, I didn't send you off with Tweed because of Malachi," he says. "I mean, we were struggling, sure, but we could have gotten along. I sent you on the road because Tweed knows the horse business. That's all you talked about back then, getting into racing. I wanted you to have every advantage in the world."

I know my father wants me to agree with him before he leaves. I know he wants me to let him know everything was okay all those years, but I can't give him that. I don't even want him to see my tears. I turn away. "I'm with better people now," I say.

"I know you are."

Without another word, my father steps out and closes the door. I wait until I'm sure he's in the stall at the end of the row. I press my face into my pillow and scream. I scream until my throat is close to bursting. It's always been easy to hate Tweed McGowan. I'd stay up late thinking of what I'd do to that guy if I ran into him when I got bigger. How I'd beat him until he was a bloody chunk of chop meat, until *he* was the one begging *me* to stop, until he swore he'd never touch another kid again.

It's a lot tougher to hate my father.

I don't even try to sleep. I spend the rest of the night listening to rain drum on the roof, listening to it roll off into puddles on the ground. I pray that every one of my horses gets scratched tomorrow on account of the sloppy track. Or better yet, that Jasper is standing in one of the shadows in the corner of my stall waiting to smother me.

No such luck.

24

EVEN AFTER SIX HOURS OF SOLID DOWNPOUR AND THE track turning into a swamp, the races go on. Riding a Thoroughbred through this mess feels more like being on an obstacle course than being on a racecourse. Water gathers along the rail in dark puddles. Long ruts and furrows litter the track. Mud splashes through the air in huge ropes and sheets. I'm covered from my jockey cap to my boots. Even with me sitting six feet up on Lily Pad's back and my head another three feet above that, my goggles are caked with crud. My head is down, and I'm riding more by feel than anything else.

I could say it's because my horse isn't a mudder. I could say it's because her hooves are bigger than spade heads and they didn't fit her for stickers, which are horseshoes made with blocks at the back so they slip less on the mud. I could blame it on not getting a minute's sleep on account of the carts of crap my father dumped on me last night. Whatever the reason, a one-legged girl on a tricycle could probably beat me by a few lengths today.

Jasper showed up at the paddock just before the race. All while I was weighing in, he was giving me that crooked-tooth grin of his from under his umbrella and twirling Spoons's tiny collar around his finger. The links were making that jingling sound I'd know anyplace — the jingling sound they made whenever Spoons would jump from rafter to rafter or turn over in that pile of rags he called a bed. I wanted to grab that collar back, but I'm sure that's exactly what Jasper was hoping for.

My father showed up too. He had Tweed under his arm and a bottle of Hedrick in his free hand. They were like two kids planning to build a clubhouse, rambling on about their strategy to land me more and more mounts for more and more money. For a guy who's never spent much time around the track, my father seems to be taking to agenting like a newborn foal takes to standing up and walking.

Lily Pad's hooves slip all over the place. They make a sucking sound each time they come up from the slop. I'm ready for her knees to buckle on account of an injury, but she keeps plodding along.

I stare at the track in front of me and let everything else, every thought that tugs at me, drop away. It's just me and Lily Pad connected by two stirrups and a thin leather strap. Rain needles at my face, but I don't turn away. The droplets streak across my goggles, but I know better than to drag a sleeve over them. A mud smear would blind me for the rest of the race. Sure it's uncomfortable, sure I'd rather be sipping lemonade on a beach someplace, but there's something about galloping through the rain on top of this horse that makes me want to stay up here and go around and around this track forever. I move forward on Lily Pad's withers and hunch closer to her mane.

From what I can see, there are three horses ahead, but there ain't no telling which ones they are. The whole lot of us are so splattered with mud that side by side we could all pass for a half dozen twins.

Mr. Standish, head trainer for Greenwillow Stables, told me Lily Pad likes to hug the rail. The trouble is with all the water pooling up over there, we have to run wide. Really wide. I brush her twice with my whip and urge her on. She tugs to the left, but I pull her back out.

We close in on the ass end of the horse in front of us. I'm not sure who's riding him—from the looks of his broad shoulders, it might be Snooker Bertley or Doc Kling. Either way, I intend to take the long way around to keep away from the deeper puddles and ruts.

The horse ahead dips. He lets out a whinny and starts skipping. A blown suspensory ligament—I'd recognize it anywhere. That pony's career is done for. Might put him down right there on the track. The jockey—it's Doc Kling—pulls up and the horse slows. It bounces and hops to keep weight off the injury. The trouble is that Lily Pad is picking up speed and closing quick. She darts to the right to avoid the collision. Her hoof slides what feels like a yard or more in the mud. Lily Pad drops almost to her knees and pops back up, nearly throwing me into the air. My boots come free from my irons. I hang on, but barely. The horses that were closing behind me move past, one on either side.

I land hard in the saddle and struggle to get my toes back in the stirrups. Once I regain my balance, I give Lily Pad every inch of reins she asks for. I encourage her to switch lead legs and give her a fair amount of whip, but this race is over with. By the time we plod across the finish line, the other horses are nearly in the next county. I'm glad my goggles are covered in mud. This way I can't see the scowls on everyone's faces.

My hands strangle the reins, and I pray for Jasper to show up with Spoons's collar still twirling around his finger. I'd use Lily Pad's spade-size hooves to trample that ugly mug so deep under the dirt that no one would bother to dig him up and give him a decent burial. Then I'd do the same to Tweed.

I yank off my goggles and scan the crowd for either one of them. Among the sea of black umbrellas, they're nowhere to be seen.

But I know they're watching.

I can feel both of their eyes on me.

I dismount and hand my reins to the handler. I unbuckle my saddle and slide it off Lily Pad's back. I storm to the scale, weigh out, and head back to the jockeys' lounge to get cleaned up.

25

"How're you doing over there, Mr. Walsh?" The bathhouse attendant eyeballs the dials on my sweatbox and nods. The name tag on his white coat says EARL.

Even though doctors say you shouldn't go longer than fifteen minutes, I've been in the sweatbox over forty-five. "Doing dandy," I manage to say.

He marks something down on his clipboard and moves along the row. Five other jockeys, one with his head lolling to the side, nod to Earl as he checks on them too. Sitting in a sweatbox to burn off weight sounds like a rough way to spend an evening, but some jockeys bury themselves neck-deep in hot manure piles. I'd rather do the sweatbox any day of the week.

There's only nineteen hours left before Fireside's big race—the Bolton Stakes—and people are already getting worked up about it. Mr. Hodge tried his best to keep Fireside's speed under wraps, but those early morning exercise sessions are open to the public, and the track's been nearly

overrun with turf writers. The papers are speculating, the
bookies are giving early odds, and anyone who recognizes me
is fishing for inside information.

Since I'll be the one on Fireside's back, I won't need to use
the sponge. I'll just take him a little wide around the turn or
tug on the reins some to slow down his momentum. Before I
know it, the race will be over and Jasper will be out of my life
forever. It still doesn't sit well with me, all this. When I first
saw Fireside, I had high hopes of winning a big-stakes race
with him one day. When they see the time I'm going to have
to run so Fireside doesn't come in the money, I'll be lucky if
Mr. Pelton doesn't send that horse off to the glue factory. But
really, what choice do I have?

Horse racing and nightlife aside, Saratoga Springs is best
known for its mineral baths. The water bubbles up out of
deep underground springs and gets pumped to one of several
fountains and bathhouses. It's loaded up with all sorts of minerals that are supposed to be good for you. People bathe in it,
drink it, you name it. Although it tastes a little like rotten
eggs, they claim it helps everything from rheumatism to liver
disease, from dyspepsia to cancer. One brochure claims it
even helps to cure "weakness of women." I'm not so sure
about that last one.

Across from me, a man lies sprawled out on a marble slab.
Attendants wearing rubber aprons massage him as they
drench him with mineral water that sprays from a row of
showerheads. Just to the right of them, a heavyset man stands
in a tile stall covering his privates as another attendant blasts
him with a high-pressure mineral-water jet. I know doctors
swear by these mineral bath treatments, but they seem damn
peculiar to me.

Even with the other jockeys and all the attendants around, I feel helpless in this sweatbox with only my head poking out the top. I can't help but think that at any moment Jasper might show up, lock me in here, and turn up the heat. No matter how much the sweat stings at my eyes, I keep them open with my hand clutched on the door handle.

"So, how's that bush-league agent working out for you?" Linus McCready asks me from the next box over.

"Tweed?" I say. "Better than a sharp stick in the eye, I suppose. I never realized how much having an agent helps."

And it's true. No matter how much I hated the idea, letting Dad and Tweed set up rides for me wasn't such a bad decision after all. My father would never know what to do if it weren't for Tweed. And with them hustling on my behalf, one on the backstretch and the other across the road at the Oklahoma Training Track, they've been able to line up more freelance rides than I ever could on my own. Having them do all that legwork has freed me up to breeze more horses every morning too. That's money in the pocket to the tune of a buck a horse. I'm hoping that once my father learns his way around this business and gets to know a good number of the trainers, we can ditch Tweed and take a run at this game by ourselves.

"Well, any time you want to move on to greener pastures, you let me know," Linus says. "My agent, Halfstep Healey, has done real good by me. He says he's looking for a good bug boy to bring on up."

"I'll give it some thought," I say, but I know I wouldn't do anything to cut my father out of his share. He's bringing in decent money on my account, and him sending cash home takes a lot of pressure off me.

I let myself bake in the sweatbox some more, until Earl comes back and turns down the dial. "An hour is more than enough for anyone," he says. "I don't know how you walking skeletons do it. Anyhow, I hear Fireside's got a hundred-and-twenty-pound impost. From the looks of it, I doubt four Shabby Jack Walshes would weigh in at one twenty."

"I'm riding a real beetle in the first," I say. "I've got to get down to a hundred and seven."

Earl shakes his head. "Don't seem right."

"You're telling me."

Earl leads me up the stairs and down the hallway to another wing. The Lincoln Bath House is huge. It's the largest bathhouse in the world and may well be the biggest building I've ever been in. The lady at reception told me they give 4,500 treatments a day in 750 tubs. Two hundred thousand a year. Amazing. The black-and-white checkerboard tiled floor, thick columns, and towering ceilings make me feel like I'm up on Mount Olympus with all those ancient Greek gods.

Earl leads me to a tiled chamber as big as a ballroom. Wide columns of light slant through the high windows and illuminate the thirty or so white tubs that line the two longer walls. Every tub is empty with the exception of a single basin, where a bath has already been drawn. I peel off my robe and slip into the warm, cloudy, beer-colored mineral water. Tiny bubbles cling to my skin. Every time I move, they fizz off me and float to the surface with a soft hiss.

"Hot water's on the left," Earl says, pointing to the faucets. "Careful turning it on, though. The spout is at the bottom near your right foot. Wouldn't want you to get scalded."

"Aces."

Earl rolls up a towel and tucks it behind my head.

"Where is everyone?" I say. "I'd have figured this place would be packed."

Earl rests a glass of water on the edge of the tub. "I thought you knew," he says. "This room has been reserved for you."

"You're kidding, right?"

"Not in the slightest."

My mind rolls through everyone I know. With all the free-lancing I've been doing, it could have been any number of people. Plenty of owners like me. Plenty of trainers like me. Heck, even the other jockeys seem to like me, and they have their own little old-boys' club that I'm probably years away from being part of. It would be nice to know who to thank, though.

"Can you tell me who?" I say.

"I'm afraid I don't know. We're closing up in a few minutes, but feel free to stay as long as you like. You've got free run of the place. Now, lie back and relax."

It's hard not to. I inhale the heat as it rises to meet my face. I rest my head on the towel and sink down until the water rises over my ears. The echoes of the room—the drip, drip, dripping—drop away. All I can hear is a slight fizzing and the occasional *whoosh* of a tub draining in one of the other rooms. I breathe deeply until the herbal mixture Earl added to the water burns the deepest parts of my nose. It's supposed to be good for sore muscles, but I don't buy into all that hocus-pocus.

Gentle hands—soft hands—begin rubbing my shoulders. I start to sit up, but the hands urge me to stay put. I sink back down. The hands roam. They move to my arms and chest first. When they start to move lower, I can't help but look.

It's Elizabeth. Her hair is pulled back, and she has a big grin plastered across her face. "I was wondering how far I could go before you opened your eyes," she says.

"I just wanted to see who it was," I say. "You know how it is being a famous jockey and all. The ladies can't help but throw themselves at me."

"Sounds to me like you're still dreaming."

"I'm just glad it wasn't Mrs. Pelton."

Elizabeth steps around to the side of the tub, and I sink as deep into the water as I can. It's a good thing the mineral water is so cloudy. Otherwise, she'd be able to see my privatest of private parts. Nonetheless, I roll away from her and lift one knee just in case.

Elizabeth is wearing a robe like mine, but she fills it much better than I do. The Lincoln Bath House is coed, but the women have their own wing, separate from the men. She's not even supposed to be in here.

"Are you the one who reserved this room?" I ask her.

"It's not as expensive as you might think. Just the price of thirty mineral baths. Less if you do it when the day is winding down and you happen to know the manager. Mind if I join you?"

"Sure." I point to the tub behind me. "Hot is on the left; cold is on the—"

"It looks so much cozier in there." She nods at my tub.

I glance toward the door to make sure no one else is around.

"Don't worry," she says. "We have the place to ourselves."

"Then what are you waiting for?"

"I'm waiting for you to shut your eyes, you lunkhead. They're as big as pie plates. I won't have you ogling me as I get in."

I close my eyes. For an instant, I consider peeking, but I figure it's not a good idea to upset a girl when she's about to get in a mineral bath with you. I cover my eyes with my hands just so she's sure I'm not sneaking a gander.

Elizabeth slips into the water next to me. It's a bit of a narrow fit, but the sides of the tub press us against each other nicely. Even though the mineral bath is already warm, her body feels hot—slippery and hot. She wraps a leg over mine and kisses me on the mouth. I turn toward her and let my free hand—the one that's not pinned down by her hip—roam along her shoulder and down her side.

"Mmmm, this feels good," she says. She rests her head back, and I kiss from her ear down her neck. My hand moves over her hip and down her thigh.

Before I know it, Elizabeth pushes up, turns around, and straddles my legs like she's boosting herself up on a pony. She sits upright, and her torso rises out of the water. The water drips down her body, and, more than anything, I want to raise my hands to her. I want to put my lips to her. I want to make her happy.

"Before we go any further," she says, "we need to be clear on something."

I'm ready for the talk about commitment. I'm ready for the talk about how she doesn't do this with just any guy. I'm ready for her to ask me if I love her—if I think we have a future together. If I think I might consider marrying her.

And the fact is that I would say or do just about anything right now to let things go further.

She tucks her blond ringlets behind both ears and locks her eyes on mine. "You *are* going to throw that race tomorrow, aren't you?" she says.

It takes me a moment to realize my jaw is hanging open. *The race? She wants to talk about the race? Now?*

Elizabeth folds an arm over her chest. "I mean, this is all about my safety," she says. "My safety and your safety. Not to mention that I already told Jane to lower the odds on Fireside. When all my girls see I'm paying out less and less on your horse, they'll start to think I know something the other bookies don't." She leans into me and smiles. "Just put me at ease and tell me you're going to throw that race. Then, I can really relax."

I can't get a word out. All I can do is stare. Stare and feel her pressing down on me. I barely nod, and Elizabeth smiles.

"I want to hear you say it, Jack."

"I'm going to throw that race," I say. "Fireside is going to lose."

"That's a good bug boy." She lowers her face to mine. Her hair falls and makes a curtain around our heads that closes out the rest of the world. She whispers, "Now let's get down to business."

26

B IG DAY," MR. HODGE SAYS. HE TAKES A LOOK AROUND the paddock at the throngs of people crowded along the fence and drinks up all the attention. He isn't usually one to care about such things, but today his barrel chest swells more than usual. "This has got to be ten times bigger than the biggest race you've run, Jack. Bigger purse than this weekend's Travers."

"Don't remind me," I say. I overheard someone mention that today's Bolton Stakes—a twelve-furlong, winner-take-all race with a twenty-thousand-dollar purse—drew more than fifteen thousand people. Fifteen thousand. That's huge. It's a larger attendance than opening day.

And I'm going to be throwing a race in front of every last one of them.

It's just a few minutes before post time, and the only horses I can think about are the ones bucking and stomping around in my gut.

After finishing up with a group of reporters, Mr. Pelton

makes his way over to us. He wraps an arm around my shoulders. His jacket smells of mothballs. "Now, now," he says. "Don't let your nerves get the best of you. How about a bicarbonate of soda to settle that stomach down?"

"I'll pass," I say.

"Big night last night, huh? That Brook can be a wild place."

It *was* a big night last night, but not on account of the Brook. I glance around for Elizabeth but can't seem to find her.

I do see a familiar face, though, and it's one that gets those horses in my gut whipped up into a stampede. It's Jasper's ugly mug, all grinning and pushed in. He's staring right at me and gives me a thumbs-up. "Looking good there, Jackie boy!" he calls. My chest pounds like it did when he was holding my head under the water.

I turn away.

Half of me wants to rush over there and tell him I'm going to do like he wants and he doesn't have to go worrying about Elizabeth. The other half of me wants to run and hide.

Mr. Hodge takes my saddle and throws it over Fireside's back. He begins to work at the undergirth. "Don't sweat this race," he says. "You've got it locked up. Break from the gate, make straight for the rail, and lead the rest of the way. None of the rest of these plugs can hold a candle to old Fireside over a mile and a half." He pats the horse on his finely dappled hindquarters, and Fireside's head picks up. His ears are pricked. He has a sleek, well-muscled chest, forearms, and shoulders, and racing dimples that show just how hard he's been training.

This horse is ready to run. This horse is ready to become a legend.

My gut knots up some more. Fireside has been working just as hard as me to get where he is—training every
day, learning the track, getting accustomed to the starting
gate—and I'm going to blow it for him. But then I remind
myself this is all about Elizabeth. She has to come first. If
Jasper did those things he said he would, I'd never forgive
myself.

Over and over again, I tell myself:

It's just one race.

It's just one race.

It's just one race.

"I know I probably don't need to ask," Mr. Hodge says,
"but you did review the lineup like I asked, didn't you?"

Most races I don't memorize anything aside from the game
plan and maybe the one or two horses to beat, but for the
Bolton Stakes I reviewed the racing form—the sheet that
outlines every pertinent detail about the horses, jockeys,
owners, and trainers—about a thousand times. I run through
each of my opponents in order, from first starting position to
last. Mr. Hodge nods his approval and gets back to prepping
Fireside.

I scan the crowd again and finally find Elizabeth. She's
wearing a green dress with a matching hat that probably gives
off more shade than one of the big oaks along the backstretch. She's standing next to Bucky, Oatmeal, and Pug, who
are all perched on the lowest rung of the fence so they can see
over. She calls to me.

I tap Mr. Hodge on the shoulder. "You mind if I go talk to
Elizabeth for a quick second?"

"Last I heard there's no difference between a quick second
and a slow one. A second's a second."

"No way," I say. "I've been running quick seconds for you all season long. It's the only reason we've won any races on those broken-down nags you call horses."

Mr. Hodge smiles. "That girl seems to be good luck for you," he says. "Go right ahead. I've got to get Fireside fitted up anyway. Damn shadow roll is sitting crooked."

Before I get over there, Oatmeal calls out: "Hot dang, those are some shiny boots! Who shined those boots up so clean, anyway? And whooee! Look at that helmet! Didja ever see a helmet sparkle like that?"

"Do me a favor, will you?" Bucky slaps Pug in the shoulder. "Give that to Oatmeal for me."

Pug slaps Oatmeal in the shoulder.

"Ouch!"

"Why don't you guys go grab a lemonade or something?" I say. "I need a moment alone with my girl."

"Alone?" Pug says, whipping his arms around. "How can you think about being alone right now? I've never seen a crowd like this before!"

"Yeah," Bucky adds. "Shabby Jack Walsh has hit the big time!"

And they're right. As soon as I come within a few feet of the fence, the crowd squeezes toward me. Dozens of arms thrust forward holding pens and programs. I start signing, hoping to clear the path to Elizabeth, but for every one I sign two appear in its place.

Finally, I wedge myself between the flailing arms, step up on the bottom rung of the fence, and give Elizabeth a hug. It's no surprise to anyone that she and I are an item, but the crowd responds with oohs and aahs like it's juicy news for the social pages.

I bury my face in her hair. "Jasper's right over there," I whisper.

Elizabeth tenses up. "Where?"

"Over my shoulder. The guy in the gray suit and the hat."

"They've *all* got gray suits and hats."

"He's right there. The guy who looks like he spent a few years as a punching bag."

"Oh, the one with the turned-in nose? Gosh, he's uglier than I imagined."

"Just keep yourself away from him."

"Hey," Elizabeth whispers back. "I want to make sure we're clear on what needs to happen. My girls have been betting on you like there isn't another week of track season left after this race. Already nearly four thousand dollars. Half to you, half to me. Sure as anything beats the five-hundred-dollar bonus they promised you for winning, huh?"

"Sure does," I say. But even as I say it, my throat tightens up, like I couldn't swallow if I wanted to.

I step off the fence, and Elizabeth backs away. My eyes connect with hers, and she gives me a wink. She squeezes her black book with the gilded edges and gives it a kiss. Before I know it, she's gone, swallowed by a sea of programs. I sign a few more and make my way back over to Mr. Hodge and Fireside. I'm the number seven horse, middle of the pack in a twelve-horse race. There's going to be a lot of traffic coming out of that gate. *Out of the gate.* And then it hits me. If I break poorly out of the gate—poorly enough to miss the lead at that first turn—I might not need to run wide or pull up at all. Everything would be less obvious.

"Riders up!" the paddock judge cries out.

Mr. Hodge gives me a leg up, and I swing my foot over

Fireside's massive, charcoal gray back. After only three weeks of racing, of being a bug boy, I feel more comfortable in the saddle than I do with my boots planted on the ground. It's like, as soon as I'm on horseback, my head clears up and I can think straight.

I glance around the picnic grounds and try to find Elizabeth. It shouldn't be hard to spot that green hat on such a tall girl. Finally, I find her near a booth where a vendor is hawking programs. She's standing with Jane and a man who has his back to me. Is it her father? I squint against the sunlight, but I can't make the guy out. He lifts a foot onto a bench, and once I see that, there's no mistaking it. He's not wearing any socks.

Jasper.

I told her to stay away from him. I even pointed him out! Everything in me wants to scream, to leap the fence with Fireside and trample Jasper into the dirt. I look to Mr. Hodge and Mr. Pelton, but I can't tell them anything. I search for Bucky, but he's disappeared. I look for my father, but he's nowhere to be seen.

Elizabeth grabs Jasper's shoulder, and I expect her to push him away. When she doesn't, I look closer. She throws her head back and laughs. It's not the kind of laugh a young lady would laugh with a stranger—or with someone she knows has threatened her. It's the kind of laugh someone might use around a relative or an old friend. Could Jasper be a business associate of her father's? My mind struggles with what I'm seeing, but with all the commotion—all the yelling and the jostling—I can't seem to comb through it. It's all tangled up in my head.

Jasper glances my way, and our eyes connect for an instant.

His smile melts away. He whispers something in Elizabeth's ear and rushes off.

I want to hop off Fireside and run over there, but I know I can't. The first horses are already making their way down the chute. Mr. Hodge calls something to me, but I don't hear a word of it. The smells of cigar smoke and freshly turned earth call to me, and I tighten my helmet strap under my chin. It's time for the post parade, and I guide Fireside behind his lead pony.

Fireside snorts and grinds his teeth. He lets out a little wheeze.

Mr. Hodge pats Fireside on the shoulder. "Remember," he says to me. "Be-Do-Achieve."

I take my whip from him and tuck it under my arm.

"Be-Do-Achieve," I say right back as Fireside and me start toward the track—seventh in a line of twelve—for the biggest race of our lives.

27

Slowing a Thoroughbred as it's trying to bolt from the starting gate is probably akin to slowing a bullet as it fires out of a rifle. When that bell sounds and those doors fly open, Fireside wants no part of me tugging back on those reins. Lucky for me, Never a Turtle, the horse to my right, makes a quick move to the inside and slams into us. Fireside grunts, stutters in his step, and almost drops to a knee. I lean to the right and struggle to stay up. And it's just enough to make my slow start believable.

The crowd—most of which has money on me since the bookies have Fireside at four to one—screams its disapproval as I drift in toward the rail behind a slew of other horses. The pack thins, and we move through our first pass of the far turn. A twelve-furlong race—a mile and a half—on a nine-furlong track is more than a lap and a quarter. We have a long way to go. I cinch in the reins a touch and find my pace right behind Track Griffin. The sounds of the grandstand get louder as we make our way toward the howling thousands.

I'll bet Jasper isn't screaming. I'll bet he's just watching, smiling so that his wrinkled-up nose wrinkles even worse.

Fireside surges beneath me. I can feel how much he wants to move to the outside and humiliate this field. He wants to break the spirit of every horse here. He tugs on the reins, asking me for permission to make the move. I deny him all the way through the straightaway and into the clubhouse turn.

"Easy, boy," I say, holding him back. "Let all those poky ponies tire themselves out."

I know it sounds strange—and people who don't ride racehorses probably wouldn't understand—but I feel guilty lying to Fireside. Sure, he's just a horse, but I'm betraying him. Fireside wants more than anything to win this race. Not just to run, but to win. It's what he was built and bred to do. It'd be like plugging a hound dog's nose or clipping a bird's wings. And here I am riding him easy, holding him back, in what is by far the biggest race of his life. This race could make his career.

Hoofbeats pound behind me. I glance back. Elevator Lover is trying to make a move on my outside. I cluck in Fireside's ear and drift to the outside of Track Griffin, which shuts the door on Elevator Lover. That is, unless Jordan Blick wants to take the long way around. He drops back to wait for a better opportunity.

"If you're not looking to win this race, step aside for someone who is!" Blick calls out.

Mr. Hodge said it to me not ten minutes ago. Be-Do-Achieve. You have to *be* the kind of person you want to *be* so that you'll *do* the things you need to *do* so you can *achieve* the things you want to *achieve*.

I want to *be* a jockey.

I've wanted to be a jockey for as long as I can remember. Holding this horse back is not doing what I need to do.

Never a Turtle, the horse that bumped me out of the gate, starts to fade. Track Griffin and Fireside drift apart to let him die out, and we pass by like he's not even moving.

Then I sit back and think on it some more. When Elizabeth and I were looking for my father down in Albany, she told me—she said it in no uncertain terms—that she had never heard of anyone named Jasper. And now she's throwing her head back, grabbing his shoulder, laughing.

Elizabeth lied to me. It's the only explanation. She lied to me to make money. She's been playing me this whole time. The two of them—Jasper and Elizabeth—are in cahoots. I'm sure of it.

She's been trying to make this race go her way all along.

It wasn't by chance that Jasper backed off just as soon as Elizabeth and I started spending time together. She had more sway over me than he ever could. Not to mention that Elizabeth agreed with Jasper's whole plan just as soon as I told her about it. She wanted me to throw this race.

But could she have gotten in that tub with me at the Lincoln Bath House all for a few dollars?

Fireside lets out another wheeze. It's louder this time, but he still seems to be running strong. I lift my head and see the lead horse, the number five, Linus McCready's mount, Galahad's Grail, a good eight lengths ahead. And there are a pack of other horses between us. I loosen the reins and give Fireside permission to step up the pace.

Each stride swallows thirty feet of track. Fireside's in the best shape of any horse I've ever ridden, and his power pounds through my legs. We leave Track Griffin behind. We pass Tempest Storm on the outside and then, at the far end of the backstretch, cut back to the rail to overtake Lucky as Loki and Humpty Dumpty on the inside.

A mile and a half seems like a long way, but on the back of a Thoroughbred, it goes by quicker than a snap. As we approach the final turn, I lift up to see what's ahead. Haberdasher, Got the Stationery, and Suki Buffalo are within two lengths, side by side by side. Ahead of them by another two and a half lengths, and stretching it out with every stride, Galahad's Grail is running strong. Linus has still got tension in the reins, and his mount's ears are pricked, so I know that horse has more to give.

I'm not sure if Fireside's got what it takes to overcome a lead like that. He's been running strong and making moves all the way down the backstretch. How much more could this horse possibly have to offer? I see a hole open between Haberdasher and Got the Stationery, but it closes down before I have a chance to take it. I could go outside, but that might spell disaster on the turn.

What choice do I have?

Just before I tell Fireside to move wide, Suki Buffalo drifts away from the rail. The gap stays open, and I go for it. I let Fireside see the hole and lean to the left so he'll change lead legs. It's a little early to change leads, but, as far as I can see, it's my only chance.

Fireside stutters for an instant. Then his strength surges. We move between Suki Buffalo and the rail, and the crowd rages. They get even louder when Suki Buffalo fades and we pull ahead.

Entering the homestretch, Galahad's Grail is still nearly four lengths up, and I know it's going to take everything Fireside has to catch him. I start with my whip and let the reins out all the way. The horse takes every inch and wheezes again. This time it feels like a raspy blast, but Fireside is running strong. He's practically begging me to run.

I let him.

At first, it looks like Galahad's Grail isn't going to let up, but finally he starts to fade. Linus McCready's arm flails wildly with his whip. Fireside inches up on the right and matches Galahad's Grail stride for stride. There is no way to describe the sound of fifteen thousand fans screaming at you. I can't hear the beating of Fireside's hooves. I can't hear myself pleading for Fireside to pour on the steam. I can't hear anything but a roar. Galahad's Grail is giving everything he's got—ears pinned, eye huge, and tongue lolling.

We cross the wire nose to nose.

Linus and I stand up in our irons.

We both know I won. It was damn close, but just like Linus eked it out in my very first outing at Saratoga, I won the Bolton Stakes by the bob of a head.

"I don't care what everyone else says," Linus calls out to me. "You've got some chops, kid!"

Before I have a chance to thank him, Fireside coughs out another raspy wheeze. His legs give out, and he drops from under me. My world turns upside down. My stomach does a somersault. My body flips around, arms and legs flailing. The crowd gasps. I let my body go limp to absorb the fall and pray Fireside doesn't land on top of me. My shoulder pounds heavy into the dirt. I hear something snap. Fireside whinnies, tumbles, and lands with a heavy thud. The other horses swerve around us and gallop past. A hoof lands in the dirt inches from my head.

I struggle to my feet. A stinging pain shoots from my neck all the way down my arm. My fingers are on fire. Dizziness grabs hold of me—a dizziness worse than any I felt when I was cutting weight, a dizziness like I never could've imagined.

I stagger to Fireside, who struggles in the dirt. Blood is streaming out both of his nostrils. He tries to lift his head, but it drops back down. His breathing is fast and shallow. He's making sounds like a deflating bagpipe, but more urgent. He tries to get his legs under him, but only manages to kick his hooves.

The next kick is weaker.

Track officials swarm around us. I see Mr. Pelton and Mr. Hodge. I see my father. A medic tries to convince me to get on a stretcher. I shake him off and drop to my knees. I bend over Fireside's massive gray head and run my good hand—the one that listens to me—along his neck. He radiates heat. Sweat froths off him. His tongue hangs out. I can see the white of his eyeball all the way around the dark part as he stares up at me, pleading.

I stare back.

Fireside lifts his head again and blows hard. His head drops heavily to the dirt, and something slithers out of his left nostril. It looks like a slug—a bloody, pus-covered slug. There's no mistaking it. Yellow and about the size of a skate wheel.

It's a sponge.

Fireside gives one last breath, and his chest sags.

And I know he's dead.

There's no doubt in my mind.

Fireside is dead.

"What happened?" Mr. Hodge barks at me. He grabs my

arm and drags me to my feet. Spikes of pain shoot through my shoulder.

"I don't know," I say.

"Tell me!" Mr. Hodge screams. The veins in his neck pulse.

"I don't know!" Tears stream from my eyes. I try to lock my gaze on Mr. Hodge's so he'll believe me, but hazy fuzz creeps in around the edges. My knees buckle, but I stay up. My guts squeeze like my stomach is trying to escape through my throat. I double over and vomit a color I've never seen before.

"Young man," one of the stewards says. "You're either going to have to go with the medics or come with us."

I can't seem to focus on him.

"I'll go with you," I say.

Everything gets blurry. Everything spins. I manage to focus on a hoofprint in the dirt. Rounded on the front, nearly straight across the back, and several inches deep. I wonder if it was made by that hoof that just missed my skull. The hoofprint starts to spin too. It rushes up at me, and everything goes black.

28

THE DOCTORS CALL IT A SEVERE CONCUSSION, AND that keeps me in the hospital a few days. I also broke my shoulder and dislocated my collarbone. Even though they're pumping me up with all sorts of medications, the pain stabs at me every time I move. The doctor said they might have to rebreak something down the road if my arm doesn't heal properly. Fat chance I'll let them do that. Lots of riders in my condition would check themselves out of the hospital and get on the next ride they could land. As for me, I'm staying off horses awhile.

When I open my eyes, Bucky is sitting in a chair beside my hospital bed. His hand is stroking my forearm just like it was when I woke up in Dr. Baumstumpf's office a few weeks back. This time, I don't pull away.

"Hey," he says.

"Hey."

"Photographers are a pain in the ass."

"Photographers?"

"The bastards are crawling all over the damn place," he says. "They're like barn rats. I caught one trying to climb a ladder and peek in through that there window. Pains in the ass, they are."

"What else has been going on?"

"God, all kinds of crap. You're big news in every paper that gives a hoot about racing, which just so happens to be all of them. This being the first season they let the bookies back inside the track, the last thing racing needed was something like this. They're talking big-time scandal here, Jack. The officials have been questioning everyone."

"Everyone?"

"All the way up to the big guy." Bucky points up toward heaven, but I know he's talking about Mr. Pelton.

"Have they questioned you?"

"Me, Oatmeal, Pug, you name it. They even questioned Niles and all the grooms."

I try to sit up, but my head spins. I lie back and rock to the side to take pressure off my shoulder. "What did you tell them?"

Bucky stares out the window. His face gets red and splotchy like he's going to burst into tears. "I had to tell them what I knew, Jack. I just had to. They said they'd ban me from the track if I didn't come clean."

Bucky keeps talking like all the words are piled up inside his mouth and they have no place to go but out.

"I need this job, Jack. I need horse racing." Tears glisten in his eyes. "I don't got anyplace else. My ma's dead on account of her protecting me from my pa. He would've killed me that night too if I didn't hide under the porch steps. I heard him pounding around the house. He was screaming my name and smashing everything he could get his mitts on." Bucky's fingers play over the keys hooked to his belt. "I locked him in the root cellar when he went for the shovel . . . and I ran to the track. I ran to the track and ain't never looked back. After Niles got questioned—after he didn't come back to the shed row—I got scared."

"Niles is gone?" I say.

"They didn't even let him get his things."

"What'd you tell them? What exactly did you say?"

"I told them about that Jasper guy you mentioned—how he doesn't wear any socks—and how he offered you two hundred bucks to throw the race."

It's got to be obvious to anyone who knows the first thing about racing that I didn't throw that race. Hell, I let Fireside win the damn thing. But my knowing Jasper was coming around the shed row with an envelope filled with dough means I knew Fireside was at risk. And now Fireside's dead. What are the stewards going to make of that? What are Mr. Pelton and Mr. Hodge going to make of that?

"Bucky—"

"What did you want me to do?" he says. The tears are flowing now. "I was afraid I'd end up on the street or riding the rails. You know what happens to those kids. Hell, Pug only rode the rails for a few months and he can't get through a night's sleep without waking up screaming." Bucky puts his hands over his face.

I know what it's like to wake up screaming. I still do the same thing myself every once in a while. After a year on the circuit with Tweed, it's hard to close my eyes without seeing that crusty toad and thinking about what he did to me.

"It's all right," I say.

"It's not all right," he cries. "I've ruined everything. I've ruined everything for all of us."

I reach over to him, but the pain jolts through my shoulder to my chest. My arm drops. "It's my fault," I say. "Don't blame yourself. I should have gone straight to Mr. Hodge. I should have gone to him the minute Jasper tried to shove that envelope into my hands."

We sit there in silence for a while. Bucky sniffles, then wipes his face with his handkerchief.

A light knock sounds on the door, and my father pokes his head in. "You're awake," he says. "The color's come back to your face. That's great." He moves behind Bucky and rests his big, rough hands on the seat back. "This boy has been sitting by your side since the accident."

"Bucky's a good friend," I say.

"Wish I had a few like that when I was growing up," my father says.

Bucky smiles through his tears. I can't help but smile back.

"Do you have any idea what it's like to see your boy fall off a horse at forty miles an hour?" my father says to me. "Do you know what it's like to watch nine other horses stampede past him? Don't ever scare me like that again, Jack."

"It doesn't look like there will be an 'again,'" I say. "No doubt I'm getting banned. Have you heard anything?"

"They're waiting to talk to you. They need your story to put all the pieces together. You know, once you're up and around." He squeezes Bucky's shoulders with two massive hands. "Hey, you mind if I talk to Jack in private for a few minutes?"

Bucky drags a sleeve across his face, and his eyes brighten. "Sure thing, Mr. Walsh. I should've figured—"

"It's okay," he says. "I only need a few minutes."

Bucky heads out. The keys hanging from his belt jingle like spurs. I don't think I'll ever look at those keys again without thinking about what they mean to Bucky—what he went through to get here.

My father slides the chair closer and sits. "I need to tell you something, Son. And I have to get it out before the officials start hitting you with all the hard questions. I'm just not quite sure how to say it."

"How about just coming right out with it?"

"I want to but—"

"Go on, then."

My father leans toward me. The white stubble on his cheeks reminds me of frost. "It was me who sponged Fireside," he says.

"What?" The word slips out before my brain has a chance to sort through what he's told me.

His head drops. "I said that I sp—"

"I heard you the first time." I try to keep my voice quiet, but it rises up on me.

"Two hundred dollars." He shakes his head. "That's a lot of money, Jack."

"Dad, I sent home more than that last week alone."

He starts playing with a frayed piece of leather on the arm of his chair. "You don't know what it's like," he says. "You don't know what it's like taking handouts from your own son." A piece of the leather tears off, and he begins rolling it between his fingers. "I feel worthless. I feel like I don't matter. That if I disappeared, everyone would get along just fine

without me—maybe better. That man, that Jasper fellow, offered me a stack of cash to fix the race, and he promised me
more opportunities down the road. He offered to get me in
on the fixes so I could win money with the bookies too. Tips
galore, he said."

I want to think about what could have been—what my life
might have been like if my father had never showed up at the
track, if he never took Jasper's money, never jammed that
sponge into Fireside's nostril. But what's the point? Fireside is
dead, and here I am holding the bag.

My throat feels like cracked leather, and my voice is the
scratchiest it's ever been. I need some water, but, instead, I
say what I need to say. "Dad, I've been breaking my ass for
over three years. I've been sending every spare dime I earned
home to you and Mom."

"What about me?" my father cries out. "I can't even pro-
vide for my own wife, my own kids! I'm a failure!" His words
echo off the walls, and I'm sure the nurses are lined up with
their ears pressed to the door.

"Your feelings ain't none of my concern," I say. "I was doing
my part. I was doing everything you asked and more. The
minute I start hitting it big you come here and screw everything up."

"I know. I know. I'm sorry." My father sucks in a deep
breath and lets it out slowly. He leans toward the bed, and his
shoulders sag. "That's why I wanted to talk to you before you
went to the officials. I want to fix this. I want to make everything right."

"It's too late," I say. "It's over."

"I'll go to the officials." His eyes plead with mine. It reminds me of that final look Fireside gave that said, *"Help me."*

"I'll tell them what I did," he says. "They can't punish you for something I did."

"Do you think anyone is going to believe you?" I say. "They're going to think you're taking the blame so I can keep on earning." I try to roll away from him, but the pain shoots through my shoulder again. "But Fireside? Why Fireside, Dad? It was the biggest race of my life. He was the best horse I ever had the chance of putting my legs around."

"I just figured—"

"You just figured you'd kill my horse. You just figured you'd destroy my career before I had a chance to do a damn thing with it."

"Watch your mouth."

"Don't you tell me to watch my mouth."

"Jack, I'm still your father."

"You could've fooled me."

"Hey!" My father rises from his seat, his face reddens, and his chest puffs out, but he looks smaller than I've ever seen him. He's not the hulking man I always remembered. He's frailer, weaker. Me, I'm lying here nearly crippled in a hospital bed and somehow I feel bigger than him.

"You stopped being my father the day you sent me off with Tweed." I jerk forward. The pain is lightning down my arm, but this time it doesn't stop me. "For two years I put up with that bastard knocking me around—no, torturing me. And why? Why did I put up with it? Because I was afraid to stand up to him . . ." Tears rise to put out the fire burning in my face. "Because where else could I go?"

"Jack, horse racing is a rough business," my father says. "Tweed was probably just toughening you up, doing what he had to do to make you into the journeyman you are today. He's brought a lot of kids into this business and—"

"Dad, Tweed raped me."

I know it's only seconds, but it feels like my father and I stare at each other for hours, days. I let time drag on until he finally says something. "Tweed? He couldn't have . . . Tweed brought you into this business. He knows the horse trade. He didn't . . ."

I don't want to argue about this. I don't want to say that word again. I don't even want that word in my head. It feels too shameful. I know I have nothing to be ashamed of. It was Tweed's doing, not mine. I've told myself that a thousand times.

But I can't escape the feeling.

There it is.

Shame.

"No," my father says. His voice is down to a whisper, and he's really rambling now. "Tweed didn't do that to you. Tweed taught you everything you know. He brought you into this business. He's brought you all kinds of work this week alone. He's teaching me—"

And the fact that my father is scrambling to find an explanation, a way not to believe what I've told him, says everything. Why should I have to argue about this at all?

"It all comes down to you, doesn't it?" I say. "It all comes down to the fact that Tweed couldn't have done all those terrible things to me because he's helping *you* make a buck. He's getting *you* out of a bind." Then, I say the hardest two words I've ever had to say to anyone:

"Get out."

"Jack . . . Son . . . No . . ."

I point to my nightstand. "There's the key to my car. It's all paid for. Take it and go."

"Jack, I want to help you. I want to make everything right."

"There's nothing you can do," I say. "I'll take the heat for this, but it's the last time. I don't want to see you again. Take the car back to Syracuse. Sell it. Go down to Belmont and get yourself another bug boy. I don't care. I've taught you how to fish, now go do it. I'll be fine on my own. Been doing it for years."

I turn away from my father just as a nurse cracks the door and leans in. "Time to try getting some food in you, sleepy-head." She opens the door the rest of the way with her hip and backs in. She wheels a cart with a covered tray on it and rolls it next to my bed.

Food. A shudder passes through me as I inhale deeply. A few months' layoff might not be the worst thing after all.

"I'll drop by later," my father says. He reaches out to touch my shoulder, but I pull away. "Maybe you'll feel better after you get something in that stomach of yours."

"No." I look him square in the eye. "No amount of food is going to make me change my mind. Take the key and go."

My father shuffles to the nightstand and places his hand on the key ring. "Jack . . ."

"Go," I say. "Get out of here."

The nurse touches my father's arm. "Mr. Walsh, Jack needs his rest."

"Get off me." My father shrugs her off and storms out. I listen to his feet stomp down the hallway. The door to the stairwell slams shut.

"Sorry about that," I say to the nurse.

"Oh, things like this can churn up a lot of old feelings," she says. "Happens all the time."

She fiddles with the corner of my bedsheet. "On a brighter note, you're being treated to a very special meal. Been keeping it warm for you." The nurse lifts the silver lid off the tray.

This is no hospital food. A huge china platter frames a generous portion of beef Wellington with scalloped potatoes and asparagus. It looks more like art than food. I'd recognize it anywhere. It's from the Brook. The smell of it goes in my nose and grabs a stranglehold on my brain. A folded card rests alongside the plate. I pick it up with my good hand and read it:

Jack,
I've been arguing with Mr. Pelton about it, but he refuses to allow you back. Get in touch after things settle down and I'll see what I can do.

All best,
Gil Hodge

"Lovely meal," the nurse says.

I pick up the silver fork. It's even heavier than it looks. I turn it around in my fingers and then place it back down. This is not the life that's meant for me, and that means leaving behind the good as well as the bad. "Take it away, will you?"

The nurse seems puzzled. "Are you sure?"

All I can manage is a nod.

"The girls at the desk are going to be fighting over this spread." She replaces the lid and pushes the cart to the door. "Can I get you anything else, Mr. Walsh?"

Mr. Walsh. No one's ever called me Mr. Walsh before. I sort of like the sound of it. I gaze out the open curtains and try not to blink on account of the tears. The late afternoon sun burns deep orange—almost red—in the western sky.

"Just the racing officials," I say. "Let them know I'm ready to talk to them."

EPILOGUE

SANTA ANITA PARK
ARCADIA, CALIFORNIA

Spring 1935

TWO YEARS.

    The racing officials suspended me from competitive riding for two years. To boot, they banned me from working Saratoga Race Course for the rest of my career.

Fireside died of an infection. It was on account of a dirty sponge. No surprise, I suppose. They buried him right there in Saratoga on the infield of Claire Court, the training track where Jasper first showed me the envelope. Where he first showed me the sponge. They refused to give Fireside a headstone—only the great Saratoga horses get headstones—but it's a beautiful place to be buried nonetheless. Hell, when I die I'd love for them to dig a hole for me there too.

At first they tried to pin everything on Niles—Niles the groom who busted Jasper's already-busted-too-many-times nose—but after I came forward and told them it was me who sponged Fireside, Niles was back grooming as soon as they could track him down. Even after I admitted to everything, the officials knew things didn't add up. Why would a guy who sponged a horse ride him hard enough to win? Why would a guy on the back of a horse need to sponge him in the first place? But they had no one else to blame. They needed a scapegoat. Fat chance it'll do any good. As long as people are running races, there will be people trying to fix them.

Even though the penalty is stiff, it's okay as far as I'm concerned. For now, I'm happy with what I've put together for myself.

I gallop Camptown Beauty past the post and enter the first turn. The mist blanketing the ground slips past us and makes it seem as though we're soaring through clouds.

I decided to head out West and start fresh. I stopped in Syracuse first to see my mom, Penny, and baby Malachi. He's the cutest little guy, looks just like my mother.

No surprise, my dad wasn't anywhere to be found.

That was fine by me. I gave Mom every spare nickel in my pocket and helped them into a nicer apartment. Married women in the workplace are frowned upon, so every morning, Mom takes off her wedding ring and heads to her job as a seamstress. She leaves the kids with my aunt who works with them on their math and reading. Between the hundreds of dollars I sent them over the past month and the fat envelope I left when I saw them, things are looking brighter than they were.

Bucky tagged along with me for the trip out West. Of course, I had to pay for his ticket. I don't know if I'll ever be able to ditch that guy. And why would I want to? He's been a real chum. He even leveled a photographer on our way out of the hospital. Knocked him out cold and smashed his camera on the sidewalk. The shutterbug threatened to sue, but what's he going to get? A stack of comics? A set of jingling keys?

I tried to convince the other boys to come with us too, but they stayed on with Mr. Pelton and Mr. Hodge. Oatmeal is lead exercise boy now, and I hear he's been clocking some pretty good times with a few of the ponies. As for Pug, well, Pug is Pug.

Santa Anita is a brand-new track—the newest in the country. When it opened this past Christmas Day, I was on the doorstep ready to handle, halterbreak, or exercise anything they could get a saddle on. I might have been suspended, but Elizabeth did help me in a strange sort of way. All that coverage in the paper made Shabby Jack Walsh a household name, just like she was aiming for it to be. Everyone around here wanted to shake my hand and hear the story of Fireside and the Bolton Stakes. And that got me plenty of breeze work.

My shoulder is healing all right. I still can't bring it all the way up and back, and it aches like a sonofabitch when I get up in the morning or when a storm is on the way. But it's getting better. Most people would say I'm crazy for going back to work so soon, but there's no place I'm more at home than in the saddle with the irons all the way up.

I guide Camptown Beauty tight against the rail and put some slack into the reins. My knees pound into my chest with each stride, and I let my thighs burn. As we enter the backstretch, I get a glimpse of the San Gabriel Mountains. They sparkle pink in the early sunlight. It's my favorite part of day, and I let my eyes roam from the track ahead of me for just a second to take it all in.

Once I started breezing full-time, I realized that it's not the race that gets my blood pumping; it's the ride. With my brief but successful record, I have no problem getting a dollar—sometimes two—for each horse I exercise. That suits me fine for now. At ten or twelve horses a day, I've got a pretty good thing going.

I'm saving up to buy a place for myself. I've had it with all the traveling and all the sleeping in the stables and all the packing up and breaking down. It's time for me to settle in. And I can't think of a nicer place than here in Arcadia.

After my father caught wind of me breezing in California, he put two and two together. He's been writing letters to me here at the track. I've read every single one, but I haven't written back. From what he tells me, he worked Belmont through the fall and then took the express down to Hialeah Park for winter and spring. He's picked up two riders, a bug boy and a full jockey, and he plans to bring them back north soon. Every letter is packed tight full of apologies, and he says he's got something important to tell me—something about what happened between him and Tweed.

The funny thing is that I don't care what happened between him and Tweed. I just want to get on with things. I just want to get a fresh start and move forward.

And that feels good.

I give Camptown Beauty a light brush with my whip, and she surges forward. It's the first time I'm breezing a horse for Mr. Meyerson, and I'm running slower than he asked me to. The closer I can pin these six furlongs to 1:10, the better chance he'll pick me up for other horses.

Camptown Beauty reaches out farther with every stride. I can feel her strength beneath me. When we charge past the final post, I know I've nailed it.

"Great time!" Mr. Meyerson calls out. I stand in the irons

and pull Camptown Beauty up. She drops into an even, re-
laxed stride, puffing and chuffing, and I move her away from
the rail to make way for any other horses that might be coming through.

After I circle back, Mr. Meyerson takes the bridle and
helps me down. "How do you little bastards do it? You're
within a fifth. Just perfect. How'd she feel?"

"Felt great," I say. "She'll be ready for next week, no problem."

"Would you put money on her?"

I unbuckle my saddle and slide it off Camptown Beauty. "I
don't bet the horses," I say. "My father taught me that."

"Sounds like your father's a smart man."

I toss my saddle over my shoulder and squint up at him.
"Same time tomorrow morning?" I ask.

"Sure thing. I'll have a few more for you to blow out."

"See you then." I tug off my helmet and goggles and make
my way to the break in the rail.

That's when I see her. She's standing like a ghost in the fog,
and, for a second, I'm not sure whether I should believe what
my eyes are telling me.

But it's her.

"Hey there," Elizabeth says. She's wearing a dark coat and a
small, dark hat—certainly not the flashy Elizabeth I know. It's
like she's aged ten years in eight months.

I drag my sleeve across my face. "Hey."

"How are you doing?"

I drape my gear over the rail. Pain lances through my
shoulder. "Not so bad," I say.

"I heard you were working out here. I was in town. Jane
got her first part."

"Good for her."

"Yeah, it's only radio, but it's with Jimmy Durante. He told her that *he's* the one who's got the face for radio—that *she* should be on the big screen. He said he'd bring her along to meet some big-time motion-picture producers one of these days."

"Super."

"So, did you read about the Brook?"

"Don't read the papers much these days."

"It burned down on New Year's Eve, a day before the accountants were coming in to audit the books, a month after it was insured for more than a hundred thousand dollars."

"That figures."

Elizabeth tucks her hair behind her ear. "Anyhow, I know you're probably busy," she says. "I just wanted to stop by and thank you."

"Thank me?"

"You know, for not ratting me out." Elizabeth stuffs her hands in her coat pockets and looks down at the dirt. "Jasper told me how you saw the two of us together. He said you were staring right through us all the way down the chute to the track."

I don't say a word.

"I was in a rough spot," she says. "I had a terrible run of luck at Belmont. I came to Saratoga nearly five grand in the red. I wasn't thinking straight. I was desperate."

"Desperate enough to send some goon after me?" I say, struggling to keep my voice from rising up. "Desperate enough to play me for a sap?"

"It was before I knew you, Jack. I know that's not a very good excuse, but once I found out he was leaning on you so hard—once we, you know, became friends—I told him to back off, that I would take care of things. I had no idea..."

I kick at the dirt with the toe of my boot.

"Look," she says. "You didn't make things so easy for me either. You promised to throw that race. All the girls bet Fireside, every one, just like I thought they would. They were betting right up until that bell rang. Sank me nearly another fifteen thousand in the hole."

"It's really not my problem," I say. I reach for my saddle, but Elizabeth goes on.

"My father kicked me out, Jack."

"He what?"

"He kicked me out." Elizabeth stuffs her hands into her coat pockets and squeezes her shoulders toward her ears. "I had to confess—to tell him what was going on. By the end of the season, I owed something close to twenty thousand dollars. There was no way I could come up with that kind of money."

"So what happened?"

"My father, he's a tough man." Elizabeth shakes her head. "You don't know him, but he's a tough man. When he took a look at my ledger, he was appalled. He said some terrible things. He sent me home to New York while he straightened things out. Paid every single girl what they were owed, right down to the last buffalo nickel. When he came home, he really let me have it."

"Can't be worse than what Jasper did to me."

"No? Well, he burned my black book in the fireplace, for one. He told me I have to play by his rules, to do what he said. He told me I couldn't go to the track ever again, and he put all sorts of other restrictions on me: who I could see, when I could see them. It was awful. Tutors came to the house, and I wasn't allowed to go out except to work at his company as a bookkeeper. A bookkeeper! He said I had to work until I paid him back. Do you know what a bookkeeper makes, Jack? Do you know how long that would take?"

"Doesn't sound to me like he kicked you out, though."

"He may as well have," Elizabeth says. "I can't live by those rules. I can't live in servitude. So, I left. What'd he think I was going to do, live like a prisoner for fifteen years? I left New York and came out here to stay with Jane."

"So, what do you want with me?"

Elizabeth moves closer. "I thought maybe . . ." She pulls her hand from her pocket. She's holding a brand-new black notebook with gilded edges. "I thought maybe we could work something out, you know? You're making some great connections on the inside here at Santa Anita, and I can work the stands. You feed me tips and I'll rope in the girls. It'll all be on the up-and-up. Fifty-fifty split."

She takes another tiny step closer. "I mean, I still care about you, Jack." She reaches a hand out to me and then draws it back. "We could try making things work out with us again too."

I lean against the rail and watch a rider gallop past on a shiny black colt. I want to be on that colt. I want to be anywhere right now other than with Elizabeth. I suck in a deep breath and fight back the tears. I don't want to give her the satisfaction of knowing that she got to me.

When I glance up, tears are finding their way down her face. "I'm so sorry," she says. "I was in a bind. I thought if I could just score big on a few races I could fix everything. This new way, we'll be equal partners, and it won't be anything more than tips here and there. It's foolproof." She puts out her hand again; it hovers inches away from me, like she's testing a hot stove. "I never meant for you to get hurt. Jasper, he used to work for my father and—"

"I don't care," I say. "It's over."

"I don't want to leave it this way, Jack. I want to make things right. I want to make things work out for us."

"No you don't," I say. "You want to make things work out for you. That's how it's been all along. You might come from money, from high society, but you're nothing more than a two-bit grifter."

"That's not—" She stops.

She sees it in my eyes.

She knows she has no chance. Not even a long shot.

Elizabeth pulls a handkerchief from her pocket and clutches it in her fingers. "So, this is it?" she says. "This is the end?"

"No," I say. "For me, it's just the beginning."

She dabs at her eyes, and her face coils up like she's holding back the biggest cry of her life. Then, she turns and walks off. Her shoulders shudder as she disappears into the fog.

Some small part of me wants to chase after her, but I tell that part to mind its own damn business. These days, I know better.

"Shabby!" a voice calls to me. I peer through the mist and see Mr. Hamilton, one of the regular trainers I ride for. "If you think you can handle it, I got a spitfire of a mare for you to blow out. Just brought her up from Mexico. She's a loaded pistol."

"There's nothing I like better!" I call back. A breeze kicks up, and something lands lightly on my boot. I look down and see Elizabeth's handkerchief, her initials, a large "E" with a smaller "R" on each side, embroidered in silver. I sling my saddle over my shoulder and head back out to the track, leaving the handkerchief in the dirt.

Another rider gallops toward me. I hear the jingling of the keys long before I see his face and I know it's Bucky. He's on a chestnut gelding with the irons raised all the way up. He cries out in delight. The rhythm of that horse's hooves is music to me. The colt puffs like a steam engine every time his lead leg strikes the ground. I still love that sound. Always will. The earthy odor of wet hay and manure fills my chest, and I know that if heaven truly is a perfect place, it looks like a racetrack as the sun burns off the mist.

ACKNOWLEDGMENTS

When I began to write this novel, I broke from the starting gate as though I was going to set all sorts of time records. When I hit the backstretch, I quickly became mired in that pesky thing called detail. Every time I found the answer to a question, six others made themselves known. History can be slippery and sticky at the same time.

This book would not have been possible without massive assistance and patience on the part of Tom Gilcoyne, Saratoga luminary and track historian; Allan Carter, historian at the National Museum of Racing and Hall of Fame (www.racing museum.org); Robert Kuhn, assistant regional director at the New York State Office of Parks, Recreation and Historic Preservation; Teri Blasko, local history librarian at the Saratoga Room at Saratoga Springs Public Library; Nick Kling, turf writer extraordinaire; Matthew Muzikar, jockey agent and go-to guy for strange questions; Rachel Muzikar, jockey, exercise rider, and my eyes on the back of a horse; James Parillo, executive director of the Historical Society of

Saratoga Springs; Howard Read, horse owner and my ticket into the Oklahoma Training Track; and Dick King, my man in the grandstands and source for the best gin and tonic on a hot day at the races. Thanks to all of you and know that any errors in this book are entirely mine.

Colossal thanks to my very special, very Dream Team of readers and critique buddies, including Loree Griffin Burns, Nancy Castaldo, Rose Kent, Liza Martz, Coleen Paratore, Leonora Scotti, and Jennifer Wolf-Kam. When there was only one set of footprints in the sand . . . well, you know the rest.

Thank you to my editor, Wesley Adams, who was excited about this horse racing book with a boy protagonist from its inception, and all the other wonderful people at Farrar, Straus and Giroux who answer my incessant and often rambling e-mails. And thanks to my agent, Linda Pratt, who grew up around horses and after reading my manuscript was amazed to find that I did not.

Finally, eternal thanks and love to my muse and two little harpies. Elaine, Ethan, and Lily—none of this happens without you.